*This wasn't a nu... bedroom.*

Jacqui turned, her intention to immediately withdraw. And found herself face-to-face with Harry Talbot, standing in front of a chest of drawers, apparently looking for underwear.

Bad enough that she'd walked into his room without even knocking, but then there was the small fact that he'd just stepped out of the shower and was naked but for a towel slung carelessly about his hips.

As he spun to face her it lost its battle with gravity.

He made no move to retrieve it and, despite opening her mouth with every intention of apologizing for having blundered into his room, she found herself quite unable to speak.

He was beautiful. Lean to the bone, hard, sculptured, his was the kind of body artists loved for their life classes.

Which made the scars lacerating his back, scars which he hadn't moved quickly enough to hide from her, all the more terrible.

Without thinking, she reached out as if to touch him, take the pain into her own body.

Just like having a heart-to-heart with your best friend,
these stories will take you from laughter to tears
and back again!

Curl up and have a

## Heart *to* Heart

with Harlequin Romance®

So heartwarming and emotional
you'll want to have some tissues handy!

Look out for more stories

in **HEART TO HEART**

coming soon to

Harlequin Romance®

# A NANNY FOR KEEPS

## Liz Fielding

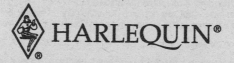

# HARLEQUIN®

TORONTO • NEW YORK • LONDON
AMSTERDAM • PARIS • SYDNEY • HAMBURG
STOCKHOLM • ATHENS • TOKYO • MILAN • MADRID
PRAGUE • WARSAW • BUDAPEST • AUCKLAND

ISBN 0-373-03872-0

A NANNY FOR KEEPS

First North American Publication 2005.

Copyright © 2005 by Liz Fielding.

This edition published by arrangement with Harlequin Books S.A.

® and TM are trademarks of the publisher. Trademarks indicated with ® are registered in the United States Patent and Trademark Office, the Canadian Trade Marks Office and in other countries.

www.eHarlequin.com

Printed in U.S.A.

# CHAPTER ONE

JACQUI MOORE peered through the low, swirling cloud, intent on keeping her precious car on the lane snaking between dry-stone walls that were much too close for comfort, and wished, not for the first time that day, that she was better at saying no.

'It's just a flying nanny job, Jacqui. A piece of cake for someone as experienced as you.'

'I'm not a nanny, flying or otherwise. Not any more.'

'A couple of hours, max,' Vickie Campbell continued, as if she hadn't spoken. 'I **wouldn**'t ask but this is an emergency and Selina Talbot is a very special client.'

'Selina Talbot?'

'Now I have your attention,' Vickie said, with satisfaction. 'You know she adopted an orphaned refugee child?'

'Yes, I've seen her photograph in *Celebrity*...'

'We supply all her staff.'

'Do you?' Jacqui jerked herself back from the brink of temptation. 'So why doesn't she have one of your wonderful nannies to take care of her little girl?'

'She does. At least she will have. I've got someone lined up, but she's on holiday—'

'Holiday! Now, there's a coincidence. You do recall that you asked me to drop by on my way to the *airport*...' she laid heavy emphasis on the word airport '...since I was passing the door anyway. You had something for me, you said,' she prompted.

5

'Oh, yes.' Vickie opened her desk drawer and handed her a padded envelope. 'The Gilchrists sent it.'

Jacqui took the envelope with its Hong Kong postmark and, heart beating like a drum as she tore it open, tipped out the contents. The supple silver links of the bracelet curled into her palm. A card fluttered to the ground.

With a feeling of dread she picked it up, turned it over and read the message.

'Jacqui?'

She shook her head, blinking furiously as she bent over her bag, pushing it out of sight. Unable for a moment to speak.

'What is it? Did the Gilchrists send you a keepsake?'

Unable to tell her exactly what the Gilchrists had done, she said, 'Something like that.'

Vickie took it from her. 'Oh, it's a charm bracelet and they've started your collection with a little heart. How sweet.' Then, 'It seems to be engraved,' she said, holding it closer to the light and squinting to read the tiny words. 'I really must get my eyes tested, but I think it says…"…*forget and smile*…".' She frowned. 'What does that mean?'

'It's a quotation from Christina Rossetti,' Jacqui said, numbly. '"Better by far you should forget and smile, Than that you should remember and be sad."'

'Oh. Yes… Well. I see.' Then, gently, 'Maybe that's good advice.'

'Yes,' she said.

'I know how much it hurt to lose her, Jacqui. She'll never forget you. Everything you did for her.'

Jacqui knew exactly what she'd done. That was why she could never take the risk again.

'Do you want me to fasten it for you?'

And because it would have looked odd if she'd stuffed it away out of sight with the card that had come with it, she allowed Vickie to fasten the chain about her wrist. Then, because she had to get out of there, she cleared her throat and said, 'Right, well, if that's all, I'd better be getting on my way.'

'Don't rush off. Your plane doesn't leave for hours.' Vickie smiled. One of those full-blooded, come on, I understand that you were upset, but it's time to move on, smiles. 'And, since you're flying by a no-frills airline from some airport in the back of beyond, you undoubtedly need the money. You haven't worked for months.'

'I haven't worked for *you* for months,' she corrected. 'Which was quite intentional. But I have been working as a temp in a jolly nice office. Regular hours, no weekends and the money isn't bad, either.'

Vickie rolled her eyes in a give-me-strength look, not fooled for a minute.

OK, 'jolly' probably overstated it.

'They've asked me to stay on,' she said. 'Permanently.'

'It's not even as if you'll have to put yourself out,' Vickie continued, treating this statement with the contempt it probably deserved and completely ignoring it.

Jacqui had done a very good job for her temporary employers, doing all the dull, repetitive jobs that no one else wanted and doing them well. She'd hated every minute of it, but it was her penance and for six months she'd punished herself. But it hadn't helped. She was going to have to try something different and maybe her family were right, a couple of weeks on her own, with no pressures, would give her time to decide what she was going to do with the rest of her life.

'You practically pass the house,' Vickie persisted, crashing into her thoughts and forcing her to concentrate on the immediate problem. But then she hadn't attracted all those *crème-de-la-crème* clients by allowing herself to be put off at the first obstacle.

'Is that so? The motorway runs right through Little Hinton, does it?'

'Not exactly through it,' she admitted, 'but it's a very minor diversion. The village is no more than five miles from the nearest exit.'

'Five? Would that be as the crow flies?'

'Six at the most. I can show you on the map.'

'Thanks, but I'll pass.'

'OK, OK, I'll be totally honest with you—'

'That would make a nice change.'

'I'm counting on you.' Oh, help... 'Selina Talbot will be arriving at any moment and it could be hours before I can find someone else to do this for me.'

'If you go in for Machiavellian subterfuge, Vickie, you should always have a back-up plan.'

'Please. It's only a little job and you wouldn't want to leave a small child here, in my office, bored to tears, would you?'

She pressed her hand over the chain on her wrist until it dug in painfully. 'I could live with it,' she said. 'Whether you could is another matter.'

'Please, Jacqui. I've got meetings, interviews—'

'And an office full of your own staff—'

'Who are all fully occupied on vital work. Just drop Maisie off at her grandmother's house and then you can head for the sun and spend the next two weeks without a thought for the rest of us slaving away in the cold and rain.'

'You think you can make me feel guilty?' she enquired, with every appearance of carelessness.

The holiday hadn't been her idea. It was her family who kept insisting that she needed a break. Not that she needed telling. She had to face herself in the mirror every morning. Vickie, she suspected, thought she knew better and had manufactured this 'crisis' purely for her benefit. It was about as blatant a piece of in-at-the-deep-end amateur psychology as she'd ever witnessed and it would serve her right if she walked out and left her lumbered with a spoilt brat causing chaos in her well-run office.

'I'll pay you double—'

'That *is* desperate.'

'—and when you come back,' Vickie continued, as if she hadn't spoken, 'we can have a little chat about your future.'

'I don't have a future,' she declared forcefully, cutting her off before this whole thing got completely out of hand.

She'd only agreed to come into the office on her way to the airport because it gave her the perfect chance to tell Vickie face-to-face that she must remove her from her books once and for all. Finally. Irrevocably. Put a stop to the tempting little job offers that she kept leaving on her answering machine.

At least in Spain she'd be safe from these sneaky little raids on her determination.

'Not as a nanny,' she said as she headed for the door. 'I'll send you a postcard—'

Vickie leapt to her feet but before she could fling herself between Jacqui and freedom, Selina Talbot swept in; tall, golden and clearly worth every cent of the millions of dollars she earned as a supermodel. The fortune she was paid as the face of a famous cosmetic company.

Maisie, her six-year-old adopted daughter—familiar from endless full-colour 'happy family' spreads in life-style magazines and the object of Vickie's unsubtle strategic planning—was at her side.

The little girl was not wearing the wash-and-wear clothes any sensible nanny would have dressed her in for travelling. Instead she was togged out in the full fairy-princess kit: a white, full-skirted voile dress with a mauve satin sash, opaque white tights and satin Mary Janes, the perfect foil for her beautiful chocolate-dark skin. A sparkly tiara perched on top of her jet curls completed the picture. Only the wings were missing.

One of her hands was in fingertip contact with her mother. From the other dangled a small white linen tote bag on which the words 'Maisie's Stuff' had been appliquéd in the same mauve satin as her sash.

The designer's logo embroidered in the same colour suggested that the outfit was a one-off creation for his favourite model's little girl.

Most small girls of her acquaintance—and she'd known enough to be certain of this—would have been crumpled and grubby within five minutes of being dressed in such an outfit.

Not Maisie Talbot. She looked like an exquisite doll. One of those collector's editions that was kept in a glass case so it wouldn't get spoiled by sticky fingers.

Most children faced with the prospect of being left in the care of complete strangers—and once again Jacqui had plenty of experience as a flying nanny to back up her theory—would have been clinging tear-fully to their mother at this point.

Maisie remained still, silent and composed as Selina

Talbot air-kissed her daughter from about three feet above her head and—having acknowledged Vickie's introduction to *'Jacqui Moore, the very experienced nanny I told you about'* by the simple expedient of handing over the matching white holdall that contained her daughter's belongings—departed with an unnerving lack of maternal fuss.

A tug of something very like compassion for this doll-child slipped beneath Jacqui's defences; a dangerous urge to pick her up and give her a cuddle. The impulse was stillborn as Maisie's dark eyes met hers and, with all the poised hauteur of her mother on a Paris catwalk, warned her not to think of doing any such thing.

Then, having firmly established a *cordon sanitaire* about her person, Maisie said, 'I'd like to go now, Jacqui.' And headed for the door, where she waited for someone to open it for her.

Vickie Campbell mouthed the words 'please' as Maisie tapped her foot impatiently and Jacqui was sorely tempted to walk away, leaving Vickie to deal with the fallout. It wasn't Vickie's mute appeal that made the difference. She just couldn't bring herself to reject a child who, despite her cool, in-charge exterior, seemed very much alone.

And she *was* practically passing the door.

'You owe me, Vickie,' she said, surrendering, helpless in the face of this two-pronged attack.

'Big time,' Vickie replied, with a grin that had better be of relief. 'Come and see me when you get back and I'll have the kind of job waiting for you that will make you drool.'

Aaah… She'd nearly fallen into the carefully set trap. Once money had exchanged hands…

'On second thoughts, have this one on me,' she replied. Then, giving her full attention to her unexpected charge, she said, 'OK, Maisie, let's go before my car gets clamped.'

'Is this it?' the child demanded, unimpressed, as they reached the street and she was confronted by a much cherished, but admittedly past its best, VW Beetle.

'This is my car,' Jacqui agreed, opening the door.

'I never travel in anything but a Mercedes.'

At which point she began to understand Vickie's anxiety not to be left alone with Miss Maisie Talbot for any length of time.

'This is a Mercedes,' she said, briskly.

'It doesn't look like one.'

'No? Well, it's a dress-down-at-work day.'

Maisie's little forehead wrinkled as she considered this outrageous statement. Then she asked, 'What's a dress-down-at-work day?'

It was too late to wish she'd kept her mouth shut. Something to bear in mind, though, next time she thought of being smart with a six-year-old.

'It's a day when you're allowed to go into work wearing jeans instead of a suit,' she explained.

'Why would anyone want to do that?'

'For fun?' she offered. Then, because Maisie's idea of fun was dressing up, not down, 'OK, well, sometimes, to raise money for charity, grown-ups pay for the pleasure of wearing whatever they want to work. Wouldn't you like to wear your princess outfit to school instead of your uniform *and* raise some money for a good cause at the same time?'

'I don't go to school.'

'You don't?'

'I have a home tutor.' Then, 'Is that why you're not

wearing a proper uniform? Because you're dressing down for charity?'

Jacqui, who had never worn a uniform, proper or otherwise, pretended she hadn't heard as she busied herself brushing down the back seat, retrieving a couple of toffee papers from the floor before she tossed in the white linen holdall next to her own bag and said, 'OK, Maisie, hop in and I'll buckle you up.'

Maisie stepped aboard, like a princess boarding a Rolls-Royce, and spread her skirts carefully across the seat. Only when she was satisfied with the result did she permit Jacqui to fasten her seat belt.

'So,' she said, in an effort to move the conversation along a little, make a connection. 'Are you planning to be a model when you grow up? Like Mummy?'

'Oh, please,' Maisie said, giving her a look that would have withered nettles. 'I've already done that and it's sooo boring.'

'I'd heard that,' Jacqui said, getting behind the wheel and starting the car.

'When I grow up, I'm going to be a doctor just like…'

'Like?' she prompted, checking the road and pulling out. But Maisie didn't answer, she had already got out her personal CD player from the bag containing her 'Stuff' and clamped the headphones to her ears, plainly indicating that she had no further interest in conversation.

It was fine, Jacqui told herself. She'd got used to journeys without endless kindergarten chatter. Eventually. You could get tired of making up new verses for 'The Wheels on the Bus'.

'We're nearly there, Maisie,' she said, as she took the exit from the roundabout marked Little Hinton.

'No, we're not,' Maisie replied, without bothering to look up. It certainly made a change from the more usual, 'Are we there yet…? Are we there yet…? Are we there yet…?'

But then there was nothing 'usual' about Maisie.

Unfortunately the child knew what she was talking about.

The village itself was nearer ten miles than six from the motorway, but it was easy enough to find and it certainly lived up to its name. There was a village shop with a post office, a pub, a garage and a small school, where a group of children were playing a skipping game in the playground, and a scattering of houses huddled around an untidy patch of grass masquerading as a village green. It took all of five minutes to check them all out, but it didn't come as a complete surprise to discover that High Tops was not among them.

The clue, of course, was in the name.

The village nestled in a small valley. Behind it rose a range of hills that were mostly obscured by low cloud. It didn't take a genius to work out where a house called High Tops was likely to be.

'So much for the ''minor'' in diversion,' she muttered, pulling up outside the village shop. 'You can forget the postcard, Vickie Campbell,' she muttered to herself.

'I told you we weren't nearly there,' Maisie said.

'So you did.'

'It's miles and miles and miles. Up there,' she added, pointing in the direction of the mist-covered hills.

'Thank you for that, Maisie. Please don't move while I ask for directions.'

'I know the way. I told you, it's up there.'

'Lovely. I won't be long.'

The child shrugged and clamped the headphones back in place.

'High Tops? You're going up to High Tops?' The doubtful look she received from the woman behind the shop counter was not reassuring.

'If you could just point me in the right direction?' she prompted.

'Are you expected?'

The city girl in Jacqui resisted the urge to enquire what possible business it could be of hers; this was, after all, deep in the country, where, according to folk-lore, everyone considered it their right to know every-one else's business. Besides, she really needed direc-tions.

'Yes, I'm expected,' she said.

'Oh, well, that's all right, then. Could you take their post for me?'

The woman didn't wait for her to reply, just handed her a carrier bag full of mail.

'Right, well,' she said, 'if you can give me direc-tions. I'm running a bit late.'

'All the same, you city folk. Just don't go racing up that lane. You never know what's on the road up there. I saw a llama once.' She didn't wait for an answer, which was just as well, since Jacqui couldn't hope to top a stray llama, but led the way out of the shop to point her in the right direction. 'It's simple enough. Carry along here, take the first turning left past the school and keep going until you get to the top. It's the only house up there. You can't miss it.'

'Thank you so much. You've been very helpful.'

'Just be careful how you go. The cloud's low today and that lane is so full of ruts and potholes it really isn't fit for anything but a Land Rover.' She gave the

VW a doubtful look and then did a swift double take
as she caught sight of Maisie sitting in the back. 'Is
that…?' Then, obviously deciding that it was, 'Proper
little doll, isn't she? Her mother was just the same at
that age.' Then, 'Well, obviously not the *same*…'
Perhaps realising that she was treading a dangerous
line, she said, 'She always looked like a little princess,
too. I swear if she'd fallen in a midden she'd have
come out smelling of roses.'

Jacqui thought that extremely unlikely, but didn't
say so. Instead she smiled and said, 'Well, thanks for
the directions. And the warning. I'll watch out for the
potholes. And the llama.'

She was definitely watching. Easing carefully over
another deep rut as the wipers swatted away the mois-
ture clinging to the windscreen, she gritted her teeth
and continued to inch her way up the lane in low gear.

'Nearly there,' she said reassuringly, although more
to herself than Maisie, who was ignoring the jolting
with as much composure as a duchess. A lot more composure than she felt, as the bottom of the car ground
on the edge of a deep, water-filled pothole that
stretched most of the way across the lane. A broken
exhaust was the last thing she needed.

The torture continued for another half a mile, ratch-
eting up the tension and tightening her shoulders.
Finally, when she was beginning to think that she must
have missed the house in the mist or that she'd taken
the wrong lane altogether, an old, lichen-encrusted gate
that looked as if it hadn't been opened in years loomed
out of nowhere, blocking the way. On it were two
signs. One might have once said 'High Tops' but was
so old that only the odd letter was still clear enough to
read. The other was new. It read 'Keep Out'.

She climbed out, and doing her best to avoid the mud and puddles, lifted the heavy metal closure and put her weight behind it, anticipating resistance...and very nearly fell flat on her face as it swung back on well-oiled hinges.

Maisie didn't say a word as Jacqui scraped the mud off her shoes and climbed back behind the wheel, apparently still totally enraptured by the CD she was listening to. But she was wearing a thoroughly self-satisfied little smile that betrayed exactly what she was thinking:

Little Princess, 1—Dumb Adult, 0.

Jacqui put the car into gear and a hundred yards or so further on the shadowy outline of a massive, ivy-clad stone house, towers at each corner, the crenellated roof suggesting a fortified stronghold rather than the home of someone's grandma, appeared out of the swirling mist.

Despite the fact that she'd never been anywhere near High Tops before, it looked vaguely familiar and Jacqui felt an odd sense of foreboding. It was, doubtless, caused by the combination of mist and mud.

She might not be totally in the mood for sun, sand and sangria, but given the choice she knew which option she'd choose. She almost felt sorry for Maisie.

Totally ridiculous of course, she told herself. At any moment the vast door would be flung open and the child enfolded in a loving welcome from her grandma, who must surely be looking out for them.

The door remained closed, however, and rather than expose Maisie's satin shoes to the elements unnecessarily she said, 'You'd better wait here while I ring the doorbell.'

Maisie looked as if she was about to say something, but instead she just sighed.

Jacqui was enfolded in the cold, damp air as she ran up the steps to a pair of iron-studded front doors that offered no concessions to the twenty-first century. There was nothing as remotely modern as an electric bell. Just an old-fashioned bell pull.

As she lifted her arm the silver bracelet slid down and the heart caught the light and flashed brightly. For a moment she froze, then she tugged hard on the bell pull and a long way off she heard the jangle of an old-fashioned bell.

From somewhere a dog raised its voice in a mournful howl.

Jacqui looked around nervously, half expecting a near relation of the Hound of the Baskervilles to come bounding out of the mist. Ridiculous. This was not Dartmoor... But nevertheless she shivered and, grasping the bell pull rather more firmly, she tugged it again.

Twice.

Almost before she let go there was a thud as a stiff bolt shot back. Then, as one half of the door opened, she realised why the house seemed familiar. She'd seen it—or at least something very like it—in a book of fairy stories she'd been given as a child; the one with all those terrifying tales about witches and trolls and giants.

This was the house where the big bad giant lived.

He still did.

Half an inch short of six feet—without her socks— Jacqui was tall for a woman but the man who opened the door loomed threateningly above her. OK, she was a step lower than him, but it wasn't just his height; he was broad, too, his shoulders filling the opening, and even his hair, a thick, dark, shaggy lion mane that clearly hadn't been near a pair of scissors in months, was, well, *big*. Gold eyes—which might have been attractive in any other setting—and three days' growth of beard only added to the leonine effect.

'Yes?' he demanded, discouragingly.

It was a little late to wish she'd stuck to her original plan; the one where, exhaust safely in one piece, she'd be heading down the motorway with nothing more challenging ahead of her than lying on a Spanish beach for two weeks.

Instead she did her best not to think about the giant in her book who'd scared her witless as he ground little kids bones to make his bread and, with what she hoped was a bright smile and a professional manner, she offered her hand in a friendly gesture.

'Hello. I'm Jacqui Moore.' Then, since he clearly required more information before he committed himself to a handshake, 'From the Campbell Agency?'

'Are you selling something? If you are I'm afraid you've risked your exhaust for nothing—'

'More than risked it,' she responded, a shade more testily than was professional as she let her hand drop, unshaken, to her side. There had been a throaty sound from the car's rear in those last couple of hundred yards to the house, suggesting that it hadn't quite cleared that last pothole. 'Shouldn't you do something about that lane?'

'I rather think that's my business, not yours. Be more careful on the way down.' And he stepped back and began to close the door.

For a moment she was too shocked to do or say anything. Then, as the gap narrowed, she did what any resourceful nanny would do in the same situation. She stuck out her foot. It was just as well she was wearing ankle boots beneath her jeans. If her footwear had been less substantial, it would have been crushed.

The giant looked at her foot and then at her. 'There's something else?' he enquired. 'You didn't just come to complain about the state of the lane?'

'No, I'm not a masochist, neither am I selling anything. I'm a flying nanny.'

'Really?' He opened the door a little wider, releasing her foot. She didn't move it, even when his predator's eyes took their time over a toe-to-head inspection that under any other circumstances would have invited a slap. Even if she'd been feeling that reckless, one look at the hard line of his upper lip was all it took to warn her that taking such liberties would not be wise. Finally, he shook his head. 'No. I'm not convinced. Mary Poppins wouldn't have left home without her umbrella.'

OK, that was it. She was here as a favour to Vickie, as a kindness to a child. She had other places to be and she'd just about had it with the giant.

'Could you please tell Mrs Talbot that I'm here?' she replied, in her best I'm-so-not-impressed manner. 'She is expecting me.'

'I rather doubt that,' he said. Nothing much happened to the upper lip, but a shift in his expression deepened the lines about his mouth, drawing attention to its lower, shockingly sensuous companion.

'Yes...' Momentarily mesmerised, she had to force herself to focus on the job. 'I've, um, brought Maisie...' She turned away, not so much to indicate the child as to give herself some breathing space.

The giant in her story book had never had that effect on her.

Maisie's response to this attention was to slump down further in the seat until all that could be seen of her was the sparkly little tiara.

'So I see,' the giant responded unenthusiastically after the briefest of glances and instantly losing the almost smile. 'Why?'

'To stay. Why else?'

'With Mrs Talbot?'

Now he sounded perplexed. Which might have been good, since it meant she had company, except, from the way he was looking at her—as if she were crazy—she was almost certain that it wasn't good at all.

'With Mrs Kate Talbot. Her grandmother,' she elaborated with exaggerated patience. Maybe it was because he was so tall, but it seemed to be taking an inordinately long time for a very simple message to reach his brain. 'I was engaged by the Campbell Agency, on behalf of Ms Selina Talbot, to bring her daughter to High Tops. I'm actually on rather a tight schedule so I'd be grateful if I could hand her over and get on my way.'

'I'm sure you would, but that won't be possible. I'm afraid you've had a wasted journey, Jacqui Moore.' He didn't sound one bit sorry. 'My aunt—'

'Your aunt?'

'My aunt, Mrs Talbot, Maisie's grandmother,' he responded, in blatant mockery of her own earlier explanation, 'is at present visiting her sister in New Zealand.'

'What? No...'

Jacqui took a deep breath. Obviously there was some simple misunderstanding here.

'Obviously there is some simple misunderstanding here,' she said, in an effort to convince herself. Vickie might be devious but she wasn't stupid and she took her business very seriously indeed. 'Ms Talbot brought her daughter into the office this morning. I was there when she arrived.'

'Lucky you.'

'I was simply pointing out that she wouldn't have done that if her mother was away. She must have spoken to her. Checked that it was convenient.'

'You might have done that. I would certainly have done that…'

The giant's mouth once more offered something that might have been a smile, except that this time no hint of amusement reached his eyes. The effect was rather more a lip-curl of contempt than a good-humoured chuckle. She dragged her gaze from his mouth…

'…but even as a child, Sally—Selina—had a tendency to assume her wish was her mother's command. She never did learn to ask nicely like everyone else. Perhaps when you look the way she does you don't have to.'

'But—'

'Nevertheless, on this occasion she's going to have to put her social life on the back burner and for once play at being mother for real.'

'But—'

But she was speaking to a closed door.

Harry Talbot closed the door and collapsed briefly against it, the sweat trickling down the back of his neck nothing to do with his recent battle with a recalcitrant boiler.

Damn Sally. Damn Jacqui Moore. Damn everyone…

He straightened, took slow, deep, calming breaths and turned to face the door, anticipating further irate jangling on the bell, but whatever game his family thought they were playing, he wasn't joining in.

Taking care of Sally's menagerie of rescue animals was a small price to pay for solitude. They didn't talk. Didn't ask questions. Didn't stare at him, wondering if he'd lost his mind.

Maisie was something else.

That woman was something else.

The bell, unexpectedly, remained silent, but he didn't fall into the trap of believing, hoping, that they had gone. She hadn't started her car and once she'd phoned her office for instructions he knew that Miss Jacqui Moore—who, in clinging jeans and a skimpy top that clung to curves that Mary Poppins could only dream of, looked nothing like the nannies that had graced his childhood nursery—would be back demanding refuge for her charge and a little civility for herself.

She'd have to make do with one out of two. And that only as a temporary measure.

Meanwhile he wasn't going to hang around waiting on her convenience. He had a boiler to fix.

Behind her the car door squeaked open and Jacqui turned just in time to see Maisie carefully avoiding a puddle as she eased herself to the ground.

'Maisie, stay in the car—' She needed to think. No, she needed to call Vickie. She'd have to get someone out here to take over from her...

'I have to go to the bathroom,' the child said. 'Right now.'

With some children that would mean RIGHT NOW! With others it was more in the nature of an early warning. Although she suspected that Maisie was a child who thought that everything she wanted should be handed to her RIGHT NOW, she was counting on the fact that she wouldn't wait until the last moment to announce her need for the bathroom. She wouldn't take the slightest risk of spoiling her pristine appearance.

Or maybe that was simply what she hoped, putting off the evil moment when she'd have to confront the giant again.

She regarded the bell pull with misgivings. Given the choice between giving it another tug and instructing Maisie to cross her legs, she'd have chosen the latter course. Unfortunately this wasn't about her. She was going to have to be brave. Soon…

'Just hold on for a second or two, Maisie,' she instructed, aware that any sign of weakness would be taken advantage of, then, pushing a strand of damp hair off her cheek and shivering a little as the cold mist seeped into her clothes, she dug her mobile out of her bag and punched in the office number. Before she bearded the giant again, she wanted to speak to Vickie and find out what the heck was going on.

'And I want a drink,' Maisie added, taking no notice of the instruction to stay put.

'Please,' she corrected automatically.

Maisie sighed. 'Please.'

'There's some juice in my bag on the front seat—'

'A hot drink.'

Little Princess, 2—Dumb Adult yet to score.

But the child had a point. She was beginning to feel the need of a cup of something warming herself. And now the idea had been put into her head, she'd welcome a comfort break, too.

'Look, just give me a minute, will you? I need to make a phone call and then we'll sort something out.'

Maisie shrugged and she turned her attention back to the phone.

'Come on, come on...' she muttered impatiently, getting clammier and colder by the minute. 'You really should wait in the car, Maisie; it's colder up here and your dress will go all limp in this weather,' she said, appealing to the child's priorities.

When there was no reply she looked around and was just in time to catch a flash of white frock disappearing around the side of the house.

# CHAPTER TWO

'OH, *HECK*!'

Jacqui had no choice but to abandon the call and take off after Maisie, vaguely registering a huge paved courtyard with a stable block on the far side as she rounded the back of the house.

She finally caught up with Maisie just as she stepped through the back door, which, despite the weather, was standing wide open.

'What are you *doing*?'

'No one ever uses the front door,' Maisie said, matter-of-factly.

'They don't?'

'Of course not. I'd have told you if you'd asked me.'

And, completely untouched by the mud that seemed to be clinging liberally to her own shoes, her dress as fresh as it had been when they left the office, Maisie walked into the house as if she owned it.

Jacqui, given no choice in the matter, followed her through an extensive mud room littered with boots, umbrellas and an impressive array of waxed jackets that looked as if they'd been handed down for generations—they probably had—and into a huge farmhouse kitchen warmed by an old-fashioned solid-fuel stove.

There was a large dog basket beside it, companionably shared by a buff-coloured chicken, feathers fluffed up to keep in the heat, and two, or possibly three, silver-tabby cats. They were so entwined—and so alike—that it was impossible to tell. A large, shaggy and depressed-looking hound was lying beside it, drying his muddy paws.

But for the chicken, she might have been tempted to lie down and join him. Instead she turned to Maisie and said, 'You know, sometimes it's better not to wait until you're asked. Just in case the person who should do the asking doesn't catch on to the fact that there's a question.'

Jacqui stopped herself. Clearly this was not the kind of conversation that your average nanny had with six-year-olds in their care.

But then she was no longer a nanny.

And Maisie, who was not exactly your average six-year-old, responded with a casual shrug. 'You didn't listen when I told you I knew the way,' she pointed out. 'I didn't think you'd listen about the door.'

Why, Jacqui silently appealed to whatever deity was responsible for the welfare of lapsed nannies, was there never a midden handy when you needed one?

'Come on.' And, not hanging around to debate the matter, Maisie opened another door, leaving Jacqui with no choice but to abandon the warmth of the kitchen and follow the child into a draughty inner hall-way from which an equally draughty staircase—the kind constructed for servants to use in the days when people who lived in houses like this had servants—rose to the next floor. 'It's this way.'

'What is?' she snapped as the cold emphasised the dampness of her clothes. Then, closing her eyes and reminding herself that Maisie was only six, that she was the adult and needed to get a grip, said, 'Sorry. I didn't mean to snap.'

'S'OK.'

No, it wasn't. It was just the latest in a long series

of mistakes she'd made that day, the biggest of which had been to respond to Vickie's call. Fooling herself into believing that it would give her a chance to convince the woman that she meant it when she said she was finished as a nanny. She'd broken all the rules and she'd been punished for it, but not as hard as she was punishing herself. And then Vickie had said that she had a package for her and she'd discovered she wasn't quite as detached, or as strong as she thought.

She took a deep, calming breath, opened her eyes and discovered she'd just made mistake number umpteen, because while she wasn't paying attention Maisie had disappeared.

'Oh, terrific!'

Clearly six months working in an office had dulled her instinct for trouble. Computers didn't get into mischief, or disappear, the minute you took your eyes off them. She'd lost the precious edge that kept her in control...

Looking around, she had half a dozen doors to choose from and, picking the nearest, she opened it to find a large pantry lined with shelves and stacked with enough of the basic essentials to feed a large family for months. But no Maisie.

As she moved to the next door the phone in her hand began to squawk loudly. She glanced at it and realised that in her mad dash after the runaway princess, she hadn't stopped to disconnect her call to the office.

She put the phone to her ear and without preamble said, 'Vickie, you've got a problem...'

'Jacqui? Is that you?'

'Yes, Vickie, it's me, Jacqui,' she confirmed, opening door two on a butler's pantry. 'Jacqui,' she repeated, 'who you've sent on a fool's errand.'

Door three, slightly ajar, revealed a small and very hard-used sitting room. Two elderly cream Labradors were in possession of the sofa and from the quantity of pale hair clinging to the fabric, considered it their personal property.

'Relax, boys,' she said, in response to anxious wags from two tails. Then, returning to her theme, 'Jacqui,' she continued, since Vickie had clearly cottoned on to the fact that she was seriously irritated and had decided to let her get it all off her chest in one go without interruption, 'who will be invoicing you for a new exhaust.'

'A new exhaust!'

She'd been sure that one would get a reaction.

'Jacqui, who's stuck in the middle of nowhere with a precocious six-year-old who not only dresses like a princess, but also thinks she is one...'

At which point she stopped of her own volition as she belatedly realised what was going on.

What a simpleton!

Vickie had said that the new nanny she'd picked for Ms Selina Talbot was on holiday prior to taking up her appointment. Clearly Jacqui was the nanny she'd picked; she just hadn't told her yet, hoping that she could snare her with her wiles...

What a fool! She'd even remarked on the coincidence and still hadn't twigged. 'Take her to her grandmother's house...' That was all she'd been asked to do. Not 'take her to her grandmother'. There never had been a grandmother, not in this hemisphere anyway.

And when—shock, horror—it turned out that there was no sweet and cuddly old lady standing by to offer hearth and home, only a deeply grouchy male who wouldn't let them past the front door, Vickie was counting on Jacqui's nurturing back-up system to kick in and take over. Knew she'd abandon her holiday to look after the child until her mother returned. After all, what else could she possibly do?

'Jacqui? Are you still there.'

'Oh, yes, I'm still here, but not for much longer. I've been a bit slow on the uptake, but you've finally been rumbled, Vickie Campbell, and I'm telling you, it won't work.'

'What are you talking about?'

She sounded so innocent! As if she really hadn't a clue...

'Your devious little plan to get me back on your books, earning you money, darling, that's what! I won't do it any more, Vickie. I told you. I can't—'

'Jacqui, you seem distraught. Have you had an accident? Is Maisie all right?'

'Maisie? Excuse me? You're worried about Maisie?'

Actually, good point. Where was Maisie? She opened another door. This time it was a small, untidy office. A small, untidy, unoccupied office. She wasn't sure which of a number of feelings claimed priority: gratitude that she had so far avoided the resident ogre, irritation with Maisie for doing a disappearing act or just plain annoyance at herself for being so gullible.

'I'm worried about both of you,' Vickie said, reclaiming her attention and settling the matter. This was all her fault.

'Me too, but mostly I'm worried about missing my flight,' she said. 'It was a cheap last-minute deal and I won't get a refund from the airline. I'm giving you due warning that I'll be looking to you to make good my losses.' Then, syrup-sweet, 'I do hope Ms Selina Talbot will understand why a simple two-hour job has cost her so much.' Finally, giving up the search and resorting to lung power, she called, 'Maisie! Where are you?'

'Jacqui? Have you lost her?' Vickie was beginning to sound genuinely worried, which was marginally cheering.

'Only temporarily. I'll have her safe and sound by the time you arrive to pick her up.'

'Me? I can't pick her up, I've got a meeting with the bank...' Then, when Jacqui didn't fill the silence with reassurance, 'Where are you, exactly?'

'Exactly? I'm in the inner hallway at High Tops, Maisie is somewhere at High Tops, too, but *exactly* where I don't know. The one person who isn't at High Tops is Maisie's grandmother.'

'I don't understand. Where is she?'

'In New Zealand.'

'What's she doing in New Zealand, for heaven's sake?'

'At a guess I'd say she's having a *holiday*...'

'OK, OK, I'm sorry—'

'Don't be sorry. Be here. It'll take you an hour and a half and if you leave now there's a chance I'll make my flight and if that happens I might even forgive you. Eventually.'

'Jacqui, be reasonable. I can't leave right now—'

'I'm afraid you're going to have to. The clock's ticking. You've just wasted a minute—'

'Give me ten minutes! I'll try and get hold of Selina, find out what's going on.'

'Nice try, but I've got you sussed and I'm telling you now, there is nothing you could say, nothing you could offer that would induce me to accept a post as Maisie Talbot's nanny.'

'But—'

'The ogre was a nice touch, by the way. Where did you find him? No, don't tell me. He was left over from the local Christmas production of *Jack and the Beanstalk*. Typecasting. With that scowl he wouldn't even need make-up.'

'OK, just give the phone to a nurse so that she can tell me which hospital you're in—'

'Jacqui! Where are you? I've got my tights all twisted up…'

Maisie's yell for help from the floor above jerked her back to reality. 'High Tops, Little Hinton, Vickie. Not quite the minor diversion I was led to believe, but they'll give you directions—and submit you to the third degree—in the village shop. Just watch out for your back axle on the way up,' she advised. 'The potholes are deep and once you leave civilisation the natives aren't exactly—' as she turned for the stairs she realised that she was no longer alone. The ogre, no doubt alerted to her presence by Maisie's yell for help, was blocking her way '—welcoming.'

Jacqui prided herself on being a thoroughly modern, sensible young woman who never succumbed to nervous palpitations or fits of the vapours, whatever the provocation, but her heart noticeably lurched at his unexpected appearance—apparently out of thin air.

He just was so *physical*. So heart-poundingly *male*. So clearly irritated to find himself under invasion.

And from somewhere—she very much feared it was her own mouth—came a small, but expressive, squeak. The kind of squeak that a mouse might make on coming face-to-face with not so much a well-fed domestic moggy, as a very wild and very hungry tiger…

'You're still here,' he said, rescuing her from this bizarre train of thought. It was a statement, not a question. He clearly wasn't pleased to see her, but it was also plain that he wasn't altogether surprised.

'Maisie needed the bathroom,' she said. 'Obviously I wouldn't have just walked in, but I'm afraid she rather took matters into her own hands...' or should that have been feet? '...and used the back door.'

*'Leaving you with little choice but to follow. I'm familiar with the way she operates. She learned it from an expert.'*

'It is her grandmother's house,' Jacqui pointed out, hating the fact that she was apologising when he was the one who was behaving boorishly. Maisie had every bit as much right to be there as he did. And what *was* he doing there, anyway?

'Unfortunately,' he replied, 'as you can see, her grandmother isn't here to take care of her.'

'There's clearly been some misunderstanding.'

'That's something you'll have to take up with Sally. I'm fully occupied looking after her four-legged waifs and strays while her mother's away.'

Which answered that question.

'Yes, well, I'm doing my best,' she said, showing him the phone in her hand, giving it a little wave to indicate that her intentions were good even while she was wondering where he'd appeared from so suddenly.

Obviously she'd known he was in the house somewhere and common sense suggested that he would hear Maisie's cry for help. Not that there was a great deal of sense—common or otherwise—in evidence. But how on earth had he got behind her?

'I'll leave you to it, then. I've got something of a crisis going on down in the cellar.' And he turned away from her to push open a door that was concealed in the panelling. Beyond it a flight of worn stone steps led down beneath the house.

With her imagination working overtime and her heart doing a fair imitation of a pile driver, she didn't ask what sort of crisis. She really didn't want to know. She just wished he'd go back to it. Whatever it was.

'Jacqui! Where are you?'

The giant glanced up the stairs. 'You'd better not keep her highness waiting,' he advised, clearly recognising an imperative command when he heard it.

'No.' She backed in the direction of the stairs. 'You're right,' she said, aware that she sounded like someone attempting to soothe a beast with an uncertain temper; one who, given half a chance, would almost certainly bite. Absolutely ridiculous, of course. While he clearly wished he'd never set eyes on her, there was nothing overtly threatening in his manner. It was just the fact that he was unnervingly...*big*. And here.

Although, come to think of it, she should be grateful for that. If the house had simply been locked up, she'd have had no option but to turn straight round and drive back to London. And wave goodbye to any chance of her two weeks in the sun. Not that a rise in temperature was likely to ease her heartache, but she needed to get away from family and friends tiptoeing around her. Treating her as if someone had died.

And they could probably do with the break, too.

'I'd, um, better go and help Maisie,' she said, taking another step back. It was one too many and she stumbled against the bottom of the stairs, lost her balance and dropped her phone as she grabbed for the banister in an attempt to save herself.

Her hand closed on air but, just as she accepted that nothing could save her, the giant reached out and caught her, holding her suspended in what, despite all her misgivings, appeared to be a very safe pair of hands.

Safe…and very large.

It was utterly foolish to imagine that they were actually spanning her waist; her waist was not of the cinched-in hand-span variety, but a rather more practical model that came equipped with a pair of sensible hips useful for propping small children on. But for one giddy moment she felt as if they did and finally understood why sane, level-headed women had allowed themselves to be laced into agonisingly small corsets in pursuit of the appearance of fragility.

Gazing up into a pair of gold tiger's eyes, she felt very fragile indeed. Utter nonsense, of course, and she knew that she really should make an effort to stand up before she did untold damage to the poor man's back.

She didn't have to. He was more than capable of doing it for her and before she knew it she was upright, her face pressed against the soft wool of his shirt, immersed in the heady scents of clean laundry, fresh male sweat, hot oil…

A lot of men—and she'd worked, very briefly, for some of them—would, at this point, have taken advantage of the situation, pulling her up close to cop a cheap feel. The giant, however, wasted no time in putting clear space between them.

His very capable hands did remain firmly about her waist, but there was nothing about his manner to suggest it was anything but a precautionary measure while she regained her balance and caught her breath. Not very flattering, actually, considering it was taking a lot longer than it should have done. She put it down to the fact that it was an unusual experience to be looking up at anyone, even a man and she had to admit, as giants went, on closer inspection he was well worth looking at.

It wasn't just his extraordinary eyes, or the breadth of his shoulders, although they were built on an impressive scale. Or even his height. Now she was standing on the same level as him, his size didn't seem quite so overwhelming. It was true that even in high heels she'd still have to look up, but not that far, and for the first time since she'd outgrown all the girls in her class at school—and all the teachers—she felt as if she was in the right place. Which was madness, as he'd be the first to remind her. She should move...

Before she could put the thought into deed, he said, 'OK now?'

'Fine,' she managed, although without much conviction and he didn't immediately release her.

'Sure?'

She found herself considering a feeble whimper...

'Really,' she insisted, pulling herself together and standing up straight.

'You could do with something for your nerves, Jacqui Moore,' he said, finally letting her go.

'It's been a trying day,' she replied. It wasn't getting any better and she shivered as the damp, clinging to her clothes and hair, made itself felt.

'Any day that involves my cousin tends to be that way.' Then, 'You're cold.'

'A bit. It's the damp. The mist is very penetrating. It can't be healthy, living in a cloud.'

'There are worse places, believe me, and the hill fog does have certain advantages. Unwanted visitors, for instance, rarely outstay their welcome.'

'That I can believe and you can trust me when I say

that I've no wish to trespass on your hospitality a moment longer than necessary,' she replied stiffly. *Whatever had she been thinking of...?* 'I've got a plane to catch.'

'Then you'd better stop dithering around, falling over your own feet, and get yourself sorted out, hadn't you?'

Charming. Just charming. But then the giant in her fairy story hadn't been a bundle of laughs, either, she reminded herself. Definitely not the kind of bedtime reading she'd have inflicted on any child in her care.

'I'd better sort out Maisie before I start making phone calls,' she said, getting back to reality and making a move to retrieve her cellphone. No matter how inconvenient he found the situation, his little niece was her first priority.

He beat her to it, picking it up and handing it to her so that she got a good look at those hands. And nearly dropped it again as his long fingers brushed against hers.

'You'd better dry yourself off, too, while you're at it. You'll find plenty of towels in the bathroom.'

She tried to speak, intent on demonstrating that if his manners were lacking in polish she at least knew how to behave, but was forced to clear her throat before she could manage a simple, 'Thank you, Mr...' Which might have worked if she'd known his name. 'Mr... Um...?' she prompted.

'Talbot,' he replied.

She waited for him to elaborate. He didn't. As if she cared. She wasn't in the slightest bit interested in his given name but common civility required she call him something other than 'um', since she was clearly going to be there for longer than either of them wanted. If he preferred to keep it formal, she wasn't going to object.

'It runs in the family,' he added.

'Right,' she said, firmly resisting the temptation to point out that just because Selina was his cousin, it didn't follow that he would have the same name. She was sure he knew that and was simply taking the opportunity to renew hostilities.

Clearly he'd only saved her from falling to avoid giving her any further excuse to delay their departure. Tough. Now she was in the house she was going nowhere until she'd sorted out Maisie's immediate future.

'Well, Mr Talbot, I can only apologise for imposing on your hospitality in this way, but, since it's going to take a while to sort out this mess and disturbing you seems inevitable, I wonder if I could possibly impose on you for a cup of tea?' She waited for him to assure her that it would be no trouble. When this didn't happen, she added, 'While I go and sort out Maisie.' Then, 'Or maybe you'd rather I left you to sort her out on your own while I go and catch my plane.'

'You can't leave her here with me.'

Well, no. Obviously she couldn't do that. But was he simply uttering the panic-stricken response of a child-phobic male? Or did he know what he was talking about?

*She had to admit that he didn't sound panic-stricken. On the contrary, he sounded like a man who knew his own mind and spoke it without fear or favour. Whether he knew or cared about child-protection regulations, they weren't an issue for him; he was simply telling her the way it was.*

'You are the only close family member immediately available,' she pointed out. It made no difference, of course; she couldn't leave Maisie in his care without Selina Talbot's explicit authority. Unlike a completely irresponsible mother, the agency couldn't just dump the child and run.

This was a 'hold until relieved' situation but, with luck—and she was surely due a little luck—he might not realise that and there was a heartening pause while he appeared to weigh up the alternatives.

Then, with something that might have been a shrug, he said, 'Indian or China?'

She just about managed to keep the 'gotcha' smile from her face as she said, 'Indian, please. This is definitely a moment for bracing and cheerful, rather than fragrant and refined, don't you think?'

*She didn't hang around to find out if he agreed. Instead, having first taken the precaution of turning round so that she could look where she was going, she headed up the stairs in search of her charge.*

Maisie, hands on hips, tights in a wrinkled heap around her ankles, scowled at her from the bathroom doorway. 'Where have you *been*? I've been waiting *hours*!'

*'Actually it was minutes, but if you'd waited for me instead of disappearing—'*

'I told you I had to *go*!'

'I know you did,' she said, more gently. 'But don't disappear on me again, OK?' Then, when there was no response, 'Maisie?'

'OK,' she muttered.

'I mean it.'

'*OK*! I heard you, all right?'

'All right.'

And hopefully, having established that simple ground rule, she tugged Maisie's tights into place, then, while the child was washing her hands, took advantage of Talbot's grudging invitation to help herself to his towels, dabbing at the bits of herself that had been exposed to the elements. With luck her clothes would dry out in the warmth of the kitchen and she wouldn't catch pneumonia but, the way her day was going, she wasn't counting on it.

'OK, Maisie, let's go and see if we can sort this mess out.'

'What mess?'

'Well, your grandmother isn't here...'

'I know.'

'You do?'

'I *heard*,' she said. 'It doesn't matter. I can stay here until my mother comes home. I've got a room of my own, you know, in one of the towers. It was decorated especially for me. The walls are mauve and the curtains are lace and it looks out over the paddock where the pony and the donkeys live.' Then, 'The pony's mine.'

'Really? I had a little pony when I was your age.'

'Did you?'

'Mmm. My Little Pony was the one called Applejack. She was the orange one, with apples painted on her bottom.'

Maisie regarded her with pity. 'My pony is *real*. His name is Fudge. Would you like to meet him?'

'I don't think there's going to be time, Maisie. The thing is you need more than a room—'

'I've got more—'

'More than a room and a pony. You need someone to take care of you.'

'There's Harry...' Harry? His name was Harry?

'...and Susan—'

'Susan?' The giant had a wife? Well...great. If

Harry Talbot was married, or even if this woman was his partner, things might just work out. Always assuming Vickie could reach Selina Talbot before she left the country. 'Who's Susan?'

'She comes in every morning to clean up and stuff.'

'Oh. Great!' No! Not great. And, ditching the smile—she had absolutely nothing to smile about—said, 'Look, Maisie, obviously there's been some kind of mix-up over the arrangements, but it's nothing for you to worry about. Mrs Campbell, at the agency, is going to talk to your mother and sort something out.'

Maisie sighed. 'She won't be able to do that. My mother will be on a plane by now and you have to turn off your mobile phone when you're in a plane.'

'So you do.'

*Bedknobs and broomsticks…*

'It's a total pain, my mother says, but they mess with the electricity and if that gets messed up you can't watch the movie.'

'I can see the problem.' Actually, Jacqui was fairly sure that if the 'electricity' got messed up you wouldn't be watching anything ever again, but in view of her own imminent flight decided not to dwell on it. She had enough on her plate without worrying about some idiot deciding to phone home just for the fun of saying 'I'm on the plane…'. 'Do you know where your mother is going?'

'Of course. She's doing a fashion shoot on the Great Wall of China. That's right on the other side of the world, you know.'

'I had heard.'

'It takes forever to get there, she said.'

Not exactly forever, but it was certain that Ms Talbot wouldn't be taking personal calls before tomorrow.

Maisie looked up at her, eyes huge and very solemn, and said reassuringly, 'It's OK. You can stay and look after me.'

No! No...

'Why don't we wait and see what Mrs Campbell says?' she suggested, brushing off the ridiculous notion that this child was in on the conspiracy.

That was bordering on paranoia.

Besides, it was not that much more than two hours since her mother had dropped her off at the agency. While normal mortals would need all of that time to get to the airport and check in, she was pretty sure that for people like Selina Talbot time was infinitely more flexible and it was possible that her plane hadn't yet taken off.

'Don't you want to look after me?' Maisie demanded, reclaiming her attention.

'It isn't a question of what I want,' she said. In another time, another life—

Maisie regarded her steadily, her dark eyes wide and innocent, and said, 'Is it because I'm not my mother's own little girl? Because I'm a different colour from her?'

# CHAPTER THREE

JACQUI felt as if all the wind had been knocked out of her.

The fact that Maisie was black had been the last thing on her mind, but it was possible that her high-profile adoption by the luminous Selina Talbot had exposed her to all kinds of unpleasant remarks from the jealous, or the just plain thoughtless.

And she'd been so wrapped up in her own problems that she'd allowed herself to be fooled by this little girl's apparent self-assurance into believing her unaffected by what was happening to her.

It didn't matter a damn that the last thing in the world she needed right now was to be responsible for someone else's child. With her mother flying off on some major assignment and her grandmother on holiday on the other side of the world, it only left the giant to care for her. And that was never going to happen. Maisie needed reassurance and she was going to get it, no matter how it messed up her own plans.

'No, Maisie. It's got absolutely nothing to do with the fact that you're adopted,' she said firmly. 'It's simply that—'

Maisie lifted her head and looked straight into her eyes. 'I think that's why Harry doesn't want me,' she said.

Jacqui was shocked to the core, and her automatic response was, 'Oh, I'm sure that's not true.' But even as she said the words she remembered the way he'd looked at Maisie as she'd waited in the car. His blank, emotionless response. Remembered the way Maisie had slid down in the seat as if to hide from him.

If she'd given the matter any consideration at all, she'd have assumed that even bad-tempered giants in story books had family feelings…

OK, so she was family by adoption. Jacqui tried to remember everything she'd read about that. There had been plenty of coverage in the lifestyle magazines at the time, but precious little in the way of detail that she could recall…

Not that who Maisie was, or where she came from was any excuse for Harry Talbot's behaviour.

Harry.

The name didn't suit him at all, she decided. It had a warm, cuddly feel to it. It was the name of a man who'd give you a hug when you were miserable, tell you good stories, know the words of every single nursery rhyme. It wasn't the name of a man who'd reject a little girl because she was adopted…

Actually, she couldn't think of a name horrible enough for a man like that and she wanted to hug this little girl so hard… Show her that at least one person in the world cared what happened to her. In other words, a straight-from-the-heart emotional reaction to the situation.

Not good.

Fighting it, she folded herself up and, instead of enveloping the child in a hug, sat on the lowest step so that she was level with Maisie. Then, taking her hands, she held them in her own and in the most matter-of-fact voice she could muster, said, 'Just you listen here, Maisie Talbot. It wouldn't make one jot of difference to me if you were sky-blue-pink with green hair and purple spots, do you understand?'

Maisie regarded her steadily for long moments. Then she gave a couldn't-care-less little shrug and said, 'OK.'

Not an overwhelming endorsement of trust, but what did she expect? There were no instant results with children. Trust had to be earned. She'd just have to show the child that she was genuine and, since she suspected that glossing over the situation was not going to impress Maisie one bit, she'd start with the truth.

'You're a smart girl, so I'm not going to mince words. We've got a problem. This is the way it is. The plan was simply for me to bring you here and hand you over to your grandmother. You know that I wasn't supposed to stay here, not even for a little while, don't you?'

She shrugged again, this time staring at her shoes and refusing to meet her gaze. 'I s'pose.'

'It's not because I don't like you, it's not because you're black, it's because I'm supposed to be catching a plane in…' she glanced at her watch and realised that time was fast running out '…well, quite soon.'

'Like my mother.' It was a flat, expressionless statement that suggested she was someone else who was flying off and abandoning her. Not fair. But then, in Maisie's shoes, she probably wouldn't give a hoot about what was fair, either.

'Well, no.' Nothing like Selina Talbot, who'd be flying first class—probably with a sky bed—and would arrive in Beijing looking a lot fresher and more relaxed than she would after being crammed in like a sardine for three hours on a charter flight. 'Your mother is working, which is really, really important. I was only going as far as Spain…' already she was talking about it in the past tense '…for a holiday.'

'Oh.' She seemed momentarily crestfallen, but immediately brightened and said, 'Do you have to go to Spain? It's nice having holidays here.' Then, presumably remembering that Harry was in residence. 'Usually.'

'I'm sure it is. For you. When your grandma is here.' Then, because this didn't seem enough, somehow, 'And you've got your lovely pony to ride.'

'There are loads of other animals. We don't have any at home because London isn't a good place for them, but my mother is always rescuing them and sending them here because Grandma has loads of room. There are dogs and cats and chickens and ducks and rabbits…' Her little face suddenly lit up as she raised her hands in an expansive gesture. 'Even some donkeys that are worn out from giving children rides on a beach somewhere.' Then, 'But if you have to go…' Her little hands dropped and the bright expression faded. 'I'll understand.'

*Double bedknobs…*

'Thank you, Maisie, but I'm not going anywhere until you've got someone to take care of you, OK?'

She didn't look up, but instead jabbed one satin toe into the threadbare carpet. 'Even if it means you miss your plane?'

'Even if it means I miss my plane,' she assured her. What choice did she have?

'You promise?'

*I promise.*

Two little words that once uttered to a child must never, ever be broken. Two little words that had to be used with the utmost care and forethought because sometimes it was beyond your power to keep them...

*But Maisie was waiting anxiously for her response and the truth was that she wasn't going anywhere until she was happy with the arrangements for this child's care. It wasn't a lifetime commitment.*

'I promise, Maisie.'

'OK.' Then, 'And if you *can't* find anyone else, you'll stay and look after me until my mother comes home, won't you?'

'Did you find everything you needed?'

Jacqui didn't think she'd ever be pleased to see Harry Talbot; she wasn't, but she was very glad of the interruption and she stood up quickly.

'Yes, thank you.'

'You'd better go on through to the kitchen, then and warm up.' He looked down at the child from his great height and she thought of the men in her own family who would have swooped down, picked her up, made her laugh. 'Hello, Maisie.'

Jacqui felt Maisie's hand creep into hers as she dropped her eyes and said, 'Hello, Harry.' Then, 'Can I see Meg's puppies?'

Puppies, rabbits, donkeys and her own special pony. It was easy to see why Maisie wanted to stay here...

But what had happened to the llama?

'She's out in the stables. I'm not taking you out there dressed like that.'

'She could change,' Jacqui said. 'If you'd be kind enough to fetch her bag in from my car. It's not locked.'

Harry Talbot gave her the kind of look that warned her not to take him for a fool and said, 'I'll bring the puppies into the kitchen.' Then, while she was still try-

ing to come up with a response that was fit for the ears
of a six-year-old, he turned and walked away.

But he had made a pot of tea and there was a tempting cut-and-come-again cherry cake on the table. 'Do
you like tea, Maisie? Or would you rather have milk?'

'Tea, please. And some of Susan's cake.'

She poured out the tea, adding plenty of milk to
Maisie's cup. Then, as she was cutting the cake, her
mobile phone began to ring. It was Vickie.

She handed Maisie a plate, then, taking the phone
into the little office so that she could speak freely, she
answered the call.

'OK, Vickie, what gives?'

'I couldn't raise Selina, but I've left a voice mail
asking her to get in touch with me urgently. As soon
as she does I'll know what alternative arrangements she
wants me to make.'

'Nice try, but according to Maisie her mother is on
her way to China. It'll be tomorrow at the earliest before she'll be picking up her messages.'

'Oh...' She let slip a word that no self-respecting
nanny would ever use, not even in the privacy of her
own room.

'What's the matter, Vickie? Did you think I wouldn't
find out?'

'I swear I didn't know where she was going. This
was just a simple delivery job.' Then, *'China?'*

'Where the silk comes from,' Jacqui replied, just a
touch acerbically. 'She's going to drape herself over
the Great Wall dressed in the kind of clothes that neither of us will ever be able to afford, even in our wild-
est dreams. You must have an emergency contact.'

'Of course I do.' She cleared her throat. 'It's her
grandmother. At High Tops.'

'Oh, come on…'

'Honestly!' Then, 'Look, I really want you back on my books, you were born to take care of children, but I'm not stupid enough to think that I could trick you into it.'

'Excuse me? So why am I here?'

'OK, I'll put my hands up to being a little underhand getting you to deliver Maisie. I simply wanted to remind you what you were put on this earth for before you went off to lie on a beach to contemplate your future career path. And I admit I hung on to that package until I had the right job to tempt you—'

She wished the woman had stuffed it in a drawer and forgotten all about it.

'I could probably sue you,' she said.

'I'm sorry but I was desperate. I didn't know how else to make you see that this is what you're made for, but I'm not a fool. The last thing I want is for you to be so ticked off that you'll never even talk to me again, let alone work for the agency.'

'Then you're not doing very well, are you?'

'I can see how it must look, but you have to believe me…'

She'd think about it, but not now. This was just wasting time.

'So what's gone wrong? While the perfect mother-and-daughter spreads in the lifestyle mags might be a touch over-the-top, I can't believe that Selina Talbot is this casual about Maisie. She must have spoken to her mother before despatching the child to stay with her.'

'Frankly? I haven't a clue. Maybe her secretary or agent or one of an absolute host of minions she employs to deal with the boring details was supposed to have made the arrangements and the wires got crossed somewhere. So who's at the house now?'

'Selina's cousin and leaving her with him is not an option. I haven't seen anyone else although Maisie assures me that there's a woman who comes in every day to cook and clean.'

'And you have a plane to catch.'

'And I have a plane to catch. So where are you? I assume you're well on your way by now?' she prompted, without any real confidence. The signal was too steady, too clear to be via a hands-free car phone.

*'Jacqui, please, try and understand. If I could have got away of course I would have, but I've already had to put back a vital meeting while I try and sort this out. I won't be able to get away from the office before six at the earliest and…'*

She stopped abruptly.

*'And?'*

'Nothing.'

'Oh, right. How big a "nothing"?'

'I've been given tickets for the Covent Garden Opera by a grateful client, if you must know. It's a gala, but honestly if I could have got away in time to make any difference I would have sacrificed…'

'Stop! Please don't perjure yourself on my account. The fact of the matter is that unless the real Mary Poppins puts in an appearance in the next half an hour, I can forget two weeks with my toes up by a swimming pool. Yes?' she prompted, when there was no immediate answer.

'I'm sorry. Really. Of course Selina Talbot will reimburse you for the cost of your holiday—'

'You're very free with her money.'

'If she ever wants domestic help from this agency again, she'll pay up with a smile.'

'Yes, well, since this particular circumstance isn't likely to be covered by my holiday insurance she's going to have to, but my missed flight is the least of our problems right now, wouldn't you say? There's a little girl here and no one to take care of her.'

'You're there. And since your holiday has been wrecked, you could do worse than see the job through.'

Well, surprise, surprise.

She didn't even offer to try and find a replacement. Not that it mattered, because she'd promised Maisie that she'd stay.

'And how long is that going to be?'

'I don't actually know. I told you, this was just a delivery job, but I'll speak to Selina tomorrow. Until then, I'm in your hands, Jacqui.'

'The giant is not going to like it,' she said. 'He doesn't like company.'

'Giant? This is the man you wouldn't leave Maisie with? Are you going to be all right there? Maybe you should take Maisie to the nearest hotel until I can check him out with Selina.'

'Maisie wants to stay even though she doesn't like him, which suggests he's grouchy rather than dangerous...' Her voice petered out as she remembered his eyes, his hands, the touch of his shirt against her cheek and swallowed. There was dangerous, she thought. And then again there was dangerous... 'We'll stay out of his way as much as possible while you sort something out with Selina.'

'You're a star, Jacqui. I'll make sure your worth is reflected in the hourly rate.'

'Oh, no, you don't get me that way. I'm on holiday.

I told you six months ago that I would never do this for money ever again and I meant it.'

'But—'

'But nothing. Just concentrate on getting hold of Selina Talbot and find out what in the world she was thinking, what she's going to do about her daughter and, even more important, when she's going to be home. In the meantime I have to go and break the good news to Harry Talbot that he has house guests.'

'I owe you, Jacqui.'

Yes, you do, she thought as she clicked off the phone and looked up to find Maisie standing in the doorway, her face alight with joy as she held up a wriggling bundle of black Labrador puppy for her to see.

'Look, Jacqui! He's so cute!'

'And beautiful,' she said, crouching down beside the child and stroking his silky head with her finger. 'You match.' Her reward, as she let the puppy snuffle at her fingers, was to have Maisie lean trustingly against her. Her arm, of its own volition, reached out to encompass both child and puppy. 'What's his name?'

'I don't think he has one.'

'Well, maybe you should give some thought to that,' carefully unfurling her arm and standing up, to put a little distance between them. 'But he'll be missing his brothers and sisters.' And there was no point in putting off giving Harry Talbot the bad news. 'Meantime, I have to speak to Mr Talbot.'

'He's gone back down the cellar.' She carried the pup back to the kitchen and placed him in a basket containing a number of wiggling look-alikes. 'He's fix-ing the boiler, I expect.'

'Is he?'

'It's a waste of time. Grandma says it's definitely on the blink. It's why she…' Maisie stopped.

'Why what, Maisie?'

'Why she's going to buy a new one.'

'Oh, right.' But, grateful for this temporary reprieve, she said, 'In that case perhaps we'd better not disturb him again. I'll just go and fetch our things in from the car.'

'You could drive round to the back to save carrying them. It's what everyone else does.' Then, looking up from the wriggle of puppies, 'I thought I should tell you that in case you didn't ask.'

'Smart thinking, Maisie.'

'You can put it in the coach house if you want.'

'Maybe I'd better wait for an invitation from Harry, first.' She'd see how he reacted to the fact that she'd moved in before she started getting really pushy and helping herself to garage space. 'I won't be a minute. Don't move from that spot while I'm gone. And don't touch anything.' Then, as Maisie opened her mouth to protest, 'Except the puppies.'

'No, Jacqui.'

'Promise.'

The child looked up and smiled, and in that instant Jacqui knew that her fate was sealed. She wasn't going anywhere until Maisie had done with her.

'I promise,' she said.

Harry Talbot lifted his head as he heard the sound of a car starting, attempting to squash a lick of guilt as the throaty roar proclaimed only too loudly that its exhaust had suffered in the journey up the lane.

He'd promised his aunt he'd get it sorted while she was away. And he would. Just before she came home.

The last thing he wanted was the neighbourhood drop-ping by, being neighbourly. He'd even persuaded the postman to leave the mail at the shop for collection.

Dammit, he had come here to avoid company. Be alone. Was it too much to ask?

He slammed the wrench into the side of the boiler and then slammed it down and headed for the stairs. If Jacqui Moore drove back down the lane with her exhaust bouncing around, there'd be nothing left of it when she got to the main road.

But by the time he'd reached the front door, there was no sign of her or her car.

He listened, but couldn't hear the sound of her retreat either, which, despite the muffling effect of the mist, surprised him. He should have felt relief, but instead walked to the gate, half expecting to find her stopped a few yards down the lane.

No relief, just guilt. Tomorrow. He'd do something about it tomorrow. And in the meantime he'd call the garage in the village and have them look out for her and offer assistance.

One of the dogs—a lanky, cross-bred creature with pretensions to deer hound—joined him, in expectation of another run.

'Forget it, mutt,' he said, returning to the house, grabbing his collar to stop him taking a short cut through the front door. 'Round the back with you. Susan will kill us both if we trail mud over her polished floor.' He pulled it shut and then followed the dog around the back.

He came to an abrupt halt when he saw the VW pulled up in the courtyard. He should have realised it was too good to be true.

Jacqui Moore, alerted by the dog, who'd rushed over

to her looking for a fuss, straightened from the back seat as if caught out in a guilty act. Forgetting, for a moment, that his intention had been to stop her, that he was intent on an errand of mercy, he said, 'What the hell do you think you're doing?'

*Which was stupid, because he could see what she was doing. She was unloading the car.*

'Would you mind not using that language in front of Maisie?' she replied, passing the child a small white bag.

'I'm so sorry,' he said, moving closer, calling the dog to heel before both females were covered in mud, further delaying their departure. 'I'll rephrase the question. What the hell do you think you're doing?'

Jacqui leaned into the car, ostensibly to pick up the matching white holdall, but in reality to gain breathing space.

She understood that Harry Talbot didn't want them cluttering up his life. She understood and was sorry to be such an annoyance, but her first concern was Maisie. She hated confrontation as much as anyone, but since it was clear that she wasn't being offered a choice, she might as well get it over with. The sooner he realised that she couldn't be bullied, the sooner he'd stop.

'Take your bag inside, Maisie, and stay in the warm,' she said. And only then did she give her full attention to Harry Talbot. It wasn't that difficult. The grey wool shirt hung loosely from his shoulders suggesting that he had, however impossible it seemed, actually lost weight and muscle. That he'd once been even broader than he was now. The washed thin denims he wore still clung to powerful thighs, however, and stretched over a hollowed stomach that only emphasised...

'Well?' he demanded, bringing her sharply back to reality.

She swallowed. 'Well, Mr Talbot,' she said, trying to erase the errant thoughts from her mind. 'This is a car and this is a bag and what I'm doing is taking the latter out of the former.'

Sarcasm, Harry realised, had been a mistake.

He'd known it from the moment he'd opened his mouth. Regretted it the moment he'd opened his mouth. The fact that she was blonde, with curves in all the right places, didn't make her dumb.

Despite a full lower lip that drooped enticingly and the kind of earthy sex appeal that sent out a siren call to man's most basic instinct, she was still a nanny and nannies didn't take nonsense from anyone. As if to confirm it, she gave him a look from grey eyes as cool as her mouth was hot, leaving him in no doubt that she wasn't in the mood to take any from him.

'Why?' he demanded. It was a fair question.

'Extraordinary,' she replied, shaking her head, so that her misted hair swung in a soft invitation to touch. How long was it since he'd touched a woman's hair...?

He curled his fingers tight against his palms, but she was already leaning back inside the car to pick up a second bag.

'You don't look stupid,' she said, turning to him as she straightened.

He wasn't about to debate it. He'd already had all the conversation he could handle.

'You can't stay here.'

She smiled. 'There! I was right. You knew the answer all along.'

'I mean it.'

*'I know you do, and I'm sorry, truly. But the car is*

*damaged, Maisie is tired and, as you've already said, you can't manage her on your own.'*

'That's not what I…' He stopped, suddenly aware of a yawning chasm opening in front of him. If he declared himself more than capable of looking after one small girl—this small girl above all others—she'd walk away and leave him to do just that.

He'd come to High Tops for solitude. Peace. To seek some kind of future for himself. She had to go and take the child with her. Now.

'Didn't you say something about catching a plane?' he enquired.

'There's always another plane.' Then, putting out a hand as if to touch his arm, reassure him, 'Don't worry, Mr Talbot, we'll keep out of your way as much as possible.'

He moved before she could make contact. 'This is intolerable. I'll speak to Sally, make her see reason.'

'You'll have to stand in line,' she replied. 'There's a queue. But no one will be speaking to your cousin until tomorrow. She's on her way to China.'

'China?'

'Where the silk comes from.' They both turned to look at Maisie, who was standing in the doorway, and once she had their full attention, she gave a little shrug and said, 'That's what Jacqui said when she was on the phone, anyway.'

'You were listening?' Jacqui asked her, not angry, not accusing the child of something bad, just distractedly; Harry suspected she was trying to remember what she'd said that she wouldn't have wanted Maisie to overhear.

'No.'

Maisie looked up at her, a picture of innocence.

Something he'd seen her do a hundred times. She'd been listening...

'I was waiting until you'd finished, that's all.' With that, she turned and flounced inside. The dog followed her.

'When is Sally due to arrive,' he asked, reclaiming her nanny's attention, 'in China?'

'I have no idea,' she said, adding a carrier bag to her load, which she held in one hand as she shut the car door. 'Tomorrow some time, I would imagine. She might pick up her messages earlier if she has a stop-over. Of course it'll be the middle of the night here so she'll probably wait until the time zones connect before she calls.'

Harry doubted that the difference in time zones would stop his cousin. It would be the sure and certain knowledge that if she called home she'd be expected to do something about the mess she'd made, rather than consideration. That and the fact that the longer she delayed, the more likely it was that someone else would have sorted it out for her by the time she did call. He didn't say that.

He said, 'In other words I'm stuck with the pair of you for the night.'

'Thanks for the welcome,' she said and smiled. It wasn't a nice smile. Not the kind of smile that would make a person feel warm inside, a smile acknowledging how hard this was for him. It was a smile that suggested, in the fullness of time, he'd regret being so thoroughly ill-mannered. 'And the tea. That at least was lukewarm when I drank it. What time do you have dinner?'

'Whenever you feel like making it, Miss Moore. Tea is about as domestic as I get.' He didn't bother to cross his fingers at this blatant lie. He just wanted her to go and he didn't care what he had to do to make it happen.

She stared at him. 'Did someone programme you?'

'I'm sorry?'

'So am I, but we'll let that pass. I mean did someone take you into a laboratory and fit a chip, pre-programmed with chauvinist clichés, into your head?'

'Is that necessary?' he enquired. 'I'd always been led to believe that it was genetic.'

'That's just something mendacious men made up to avoid doing their share of the housework.'

'Possibly,' he admitted. 'Although my personal theory is that it was made up by pathetic women to excuse their inability to control them. No matter how hard they try.'

Her eyes, he noticed with interest, had heated up to the colour of molten silver, but that was the only indication that her temper was on a short fuse.

'I only asked what time you eat,' she continued, with impressive outward calm, 'so that we won't disturb you. You are, of course, more than welcome to join us for nursery tea at five o'clock.'

'You won't find any fish fingers in my freezer.'

'No? Well, I'm sure we'll manage.'

He shrugged. 'Maisie has a room of her own in the east tower,' he said, resisting his natural inclination to take the bags and carry them up for her. The worse her opinion of him, the more likely she was to keep out of his way. 'She knows where it is. You can have the room next door. Don't get comfortable, you're not staying a minute longer than necessary.'

'Extraordinary! I'd have said we didn't have a thought in common, but do you know that's exactly what I promised Maisie?' He must have frowned because she added, by way of explanation, 'That I'd only stay until we could find someone she liked to take care of her.' And she smiled again, as if she knew something that he didn't.

He ignored the smile and said, 'I'm glad to hear it. Give me your keys and I'll put your car in the coach house.'

'Oh, right,' she said, clearly caught off balance by such unexpected thoughtfulness. 'Well, thank—'

'Nothing that old should be left out overnight in the cold and damp. I'll take a look at your exhaust while I'm about it. I wouldn't want anything to delay you in the morning.'

# CHAPTER FOUR

JACQUI was shaking so much from her confrontation with Harry Talbot that her legs were jelly as she climbed the stairs.

Thankfully, Maisie was skipping along happily in front of her, leading the way up a second flight of stairs to her own special bedroom and not in the slightest bit bothered, apparently, at the lack of welcome. And hopefully not fully understanding the less than edifying exchange between them.

What on earth had she been thinking?

She'd always known that the giant wasn't going to be happy about them staying, although even she hadn't been prepared for quite such a hostile response.

Not that she'd exactly helped matters.

If Harry Talbot had been a wasp's nest, she would have been the idiot poking it. Which wasn't like her at all.

Usually she was the soul of tact. Was always prepared to see the other person's point of view. Even to the point of being walked all over—witness the way Vickie Campbell had stitched her up like a kipper...

Pouring oil on troubled waters was something she usually managed without thinking, but Harry Talbot's attitude made her see red, and instead of pouring the oil she'd set fire to it and tossed in a couple of metaphorical hand grenades for good measure.

It was within her job description to stand up to him,

if necessary, for Maisie's sake. Unfortunately she'd done rather more than that.

Not that it was entirely her fault. He had seriously provoked her.

She couldn't have made it plainer that she didn't want to stay, but honestly, from the way he'd looked at her, anyone would have thought she'd planned the whole thing just to annoy him.

As if she'd really *choose* to abandon a holiday in the sun—no matter how cheap and cheerful—in order to stay on some cold, fogbound hilltop in a less than spring-like English spring with a bad-tempered bigot.

'This is my room,' Maisie announced, opening the door, forcing her to push Harry Talbot to the back of her mind and concentrate on the job in hand.

Jacqui instantly saw the attraction; understood why the child would want to stay despite Harry Talbot's miserable attitude. The room, at the top of the tower, was pure princess fantasy, from the lace-draped little four-poster bed and matching looped-back curtains, to the hand-painted furniture, where flora in all shades through mauve to deepest purple had been relieved by a green tracery of stems and leaves.

And Harry Talbot must have fixed the boiler because the room was warm and, despite the miserable weather, the bed didn't feel in the slightest bit damp.

'It's lovely, Maisie. Did your grandmother do all this just for you?'

'Don't be silly. My mother got in a decorator.'

Of course she did. Go to the back of the class, Jacqui told herself, slapping at her own wrist as the child flounced across to the window.

'You can see Fudge's field from here.'

Jacqui, fully prepared to heap admiration on some

fat little pony, followed her, but the mist pressed against the glass, obliterating the view.

'It's not very nice out there.' Maisie frowned. 'He'll be cold.'

'Won't he be tucked up in the stables, where it's warm and dry?'

'Maybe. Can we go and make sure?'

Jacqui would have rather stayed away from the out-buildings. Harry Talbot had said he'd look at her car and she had no wish to run into him until he'd had a chance to forget some of the things she'd said. Until she'd had a chance to forget them, come to that. But somehow she didn't think that Maisie was in the habit of taking 'no' for an answer.

'Well, all right, but I think you ought to change first. Have you got anything more...' she baulked at the word 'sensible'. It seemed unlikely that Maisie knew the meaning of the word, but not even the most thoughtless mother would allow her child to ride in a frilly frock and satin shoes '...suitable? You know, for riding.'

Even as she said the word she had an image of little Bonnie Butler in *Gone With the Wind*, dressed in a velvet riding habit and ostrich feathers. Or had she just imagined the feathers...?

'Trousers, for instance?' she offered, more in hope than expectation, unzipping the child's holdall to look for herself.

The white voile dress, she discovered as she un-packed—shaking out dress after dress and putting them on the mauve satin padded hangers she found in the wardrobe—was, by Maisie's standards, restrained.

She'd even packed a pair of tiny designer fairy wings for those extra-special occasions. Embroidered and beaded in silver and the inevitable mauve. Very pretty, but not, by any stretch of the imagination, sensible.

There were no jeans. Not even a pair of designer jodhpurs or handmade boots, which would have been more Maisie's style. No trousers of any kind, in fact. No boots. No hard hat. Not even a pair of mauve, sparkly waterproof wellington boots to keep her feet dry. Just more pairs of satin slippers to match her frocks.

'There are wellingtons and coats in the mud room,' Maisie offered. 'You just try them on until you find stuff that fits.'

'Right, well, I'll just put my bag next door and we'll go and sort something out.'

'Next door' hadn't had the benefit of a decorator any time in the last fifty years if the faded floral wallpaper was anything to go by. But it was warm and, if the comfort was shabby, it was genuine.

She'd search out the linen cupboard and make both their beds later.

Petting the pony—since no matter what Maisie's views on the subject, she wouldn't even be sitting on him without a hard hat—obviously, was far more important.

Ten minutes later they were walking across the courtyard. Jacqui, well shod in ankle boots, declined to join in Maisie's hunt for a pair of wellies that fit, but she had borrowed a waxed jacket so old that all trace of wax had pretty much worn away.

The smallest one in the mud room was still too big for Maisie. With the sleeves folded back it did the job, but Jacqui had to stifle a smile at the sight of her stomping happily across the courtyard in a pair of slightly too large green wellington boots, a froth of white skirt sticking out from beneath the jacket, sparkly tiara still perched atop her dark curls.

Maisie Talbot might be precocious, but she certainly wasn't dull.

'Where are you two going?' Harry Talbot appeared in the entrance to the coach house, wiping oily hands on a rag.

'Maisie wanted to say hello to Fudge.' Why did she have to sound so defensive? 'Her pony?' she added when he didn't appear to know what she was talking about.

'That's what he's called?' His expression suggested that never had pony and name been more aptly matched. 'All right. Just don't go wandering off in this mist. It's easy to get disorientated.'

'I don't suppose there's any chance of you getting lost, is there?'

She knew she shouldn't have said that even before he stilled. Said, coldly, 'Is that your idea of a joke?'

If it was—and she wasn't prepared to examine exactly what her comment was meant to be—it had fallen distinctly flat, because he certainly wasn't laughing.

'Yes... No... I'm sorry.' And she was. 'Really.'

He used his head to indicate the far end of the yard. 'The pony's in the end stall. Don't give her sugar; she's old and her teeth can't take any more abuse. You'll find some carrots in a net on the wall.'

Maisie ran on, but Jacqui stayed put. Nothing could wipe out what, in retrospect, seemed a deeply callous remark that was completely alien to her nature, but she refused to give him the satisfaction of running away.

'What's the verdict on the car?'

'I'm no mechanic but I'd say your exhaust has taken

its last journey. I'm just going to give the garage a call. Don't worry, I'll put it on my account.'

'Thank you.'

He shrugged. 'I think you've probably suffered enough at the hands of the Talbot family for one day.' Then, 'Hadn't you better go and make sure that Maisie doesn't get trampled by her pony?'

'It wouldn't dare,' she said.

And finally got what might just have been a smile from the man.

For a moment neither of them moved.

'I'd better go and give the garage—'

'I should go and keep an eye—'

He moved first, peeling away and striding back to the house without another word. She watched him for a moment, then, jerking her hormones back into line— they had no taste—she went after Maisie.


'Did you find something? For Maisie's tea?'

Jacqui looked up from the sauce she was gently stirring on the stove. She hadn't seen Harry Talbot since he'd left her standing by the coach house. Hadn't been much relishing their next encounter, but he didn't look as if he was about to do anything particularly ogre-like.

If she could just stop herself from saying something stupid long enough to get him on her side...

'Yes, thank you. I'm making spaghetti carbonara for both of us.' Then, 'Well, penne carbonara. It's easier for little ones to manage.'

His eyebrows rose. 'Nursery tea has certainly improved since my day. The best I could hope for was macaroni cheese.'

'Nannies move with the times, just like everyone else, Mr Talbot. And so do children. Apparently it's one of her favourites and since all the ingredients were to hand...' Then, 'But I do a mean fish finger when I put my mind to it. Not the frozen variety, of course. I make my own.'

'I didn't know you could.'

The temptation to respond with some smart-alecky remark was strong, but she restrained herself. Maisie wanted to stay here and making him angry wasn't helping her cause.

'You probably call them goujons. And pay an exorbitant price for them in restaurants.' Not that he looked as if he was in the habit of frequenting expensive restaurants. 'Are you hungry?' she asked, concentrating on the sauce, so that she didn't have to look at him. 'I've made more of this than we can eat.' And, since she didn't want him to refuse, she gave him an escape route. 'I'll leave a dish in the fridge for you to heat up when we're out of your way if you prefer.'

She sensed that he was hesitating. Caught between the desire to eat something he hadn't poured out of a tin—and since the pantry was full of tins, she was pretty sure that was what he'd been doing—and telling her to get lost.

But all he said was, 'Thank you.'

It wasn't exactly disappointment that made her heart sink. But she had, for just a moment, hoped that he might pull out a chair, sit down at the table and join them. Imagined a little bonding between Maisie and Harry over the comfort food, with her playing the good fairy.

Pathetic.

Maisie was the only one around here with wings.

Although he was still in the kitchen. She was giving

her entire attention to the sauce, but she could feel him behind her.

'You'll find ice cream in the pantry freezer, if Maisie wants some,' he said. 'Unless, of course, you've managed to whip up some fancy pudding as well?'

He'd almost been nice there. Almost. For a moment. She was going to reward him with a smile, but when she turned round, he'd gone.

She bathed Maisie and got her ready for bed, tucking her in with a teddy and reading her a story from one of the many books on the shelf. A jolly story about a little bear's bedtime. Nothing to cause nightmares.

She was asleep before little bear, and Jacqui sat there for a while, watching her breathing. Smoothed the cover. Turned the light down until it was little more than a glow.

Somewhere, on the other side of the world, another child would soon be starting a new day. Crumpled and grumpy from sleep, reaching out for a cuddle from another woman…

She blinked fiercely, touching the bracelet as she swallowed down the ache. A bath. She needed to soak in warm, lavender-scented water. Forget and smile. Not even remotely possible, but maybe she should try concentrating on the joy, rather than the heartache…

Since she was travelling light and hadn't bothered with a bathrobe, she helped herself to a robe hanging behind the bedroom door before going down to the kitchen to make herself something warm to drink.

Only the concealed lighting above the worktops was switched on, leaving the centre of the room barely lit. The chicken stirred and clucked disapprovingly from the basket. She gave it a wide berth. She didn't much like chickens—even when they were house pets.

The cats didn't twitch more than a whisker. It was the dog, always hopeful of food, slithering across the quarry-tiled floor that made her turn.

Harry Talbot had apparently been sitting at the kitchen table, finishing his supper. Now he was on his feet and it was a moot point which of them was most surprised.

'I'm sorry,' she said. 'I thought you'd be long finished.'

'Yes, well, I would have been but those wretched donkeys don't know when they're well off. The ungrateful little beasts made a mass dash for freedom when I went out to feed them,' he said, pushing back the chair. 'By the I'd time I'd rounded them all up I was plastered with mud.'

Which explained why his dark hair was now slickly combed back, although where it was drying it was already beginning to spring back into an unruly mop of curls. Why he was wearing fresh jeans and a dark blue collarless shirt. And looked good enough to eat himself.

'What about the llama?' she asked. 'Is that an ungrateful beast, too?'

'Who told you about the llama?'

'The woman in the village shop warned me to watch out for it on the road.'

'It was looking for company. Kate found it a home with a small herd on the other side of the valley.'

'Oh. I thought she'd made it up.'

'I wish.' Then, 'Well?' he demanded, when she didn't move. 'What do you want?'

'Nothing. At least, I'll come back. I don't want to disturb you.'

'You already have, so you might as well make a proper job of it. What do you want?' he repeated.

Nothing different about his manners, then. They were just the same.

'I was going to make myself a hot drink and take it upstairs.'

'Do whatever you like. I've finished,' he said, abandoning his half-eaten meal and making a move to leave.

'Can I make you something?' she asked, feeling dreadful about interrupting his meal even though she had, moments before, been wishing it would choke him. It was only polite to make the offer. One of them should probably make the effort and it clearly wasn't going to be him.

'Playing the domestic goddess isn't going to change my mind, Miss Moore,' he replied, as if to prove her point. 'I'm quite capable of making my own coffee.'

'Obviously you'd have to be,' she replied, 'or go without.'

So much for politeness. She'd been so determined not to let him annoy her, but apparently all he had to do was speak...

'I'm actually making tea,' she continued, in an effort at appeasement. After all, she had not only matched his rudeness, but also trumped it. 'However, while acknowledging your undoubted competence, it would be no trouble to make you a pot of coffee at the same time. Since I'm boiling the kettle anyway. You can come back when I've gone upstairs and help yourself if you don't want to stay.'

There was a moment of absolute silence when the

air was thick with words waiting to be spoken. Not even the dog moved.

Harry felt as if his feet were welded to the floor. His brain was urging him to walk out. He couldn't handle people. Couldn't handle this woman who one minute was all soft curves and temptation, and the next disapproval and a sharp tongue. It was too complex. Too difficult. His only thoughts had, for so long, been simple, one-dimensional, fixed on survival, locked on one goal because he'd known that if he lost sight of it, even for a moment, he'd lose his mind.

He had to be alone. It was the only way he could survive...

But his body, which he'd been driving so hard and so long on sheer will-power, seemed suddenly unable to carry out the simplest of commands. It had demanded the food she cooked and now he seemed unable to walk away; trapped between the possibility of heaven and the certainty of hell.

As Jacqui waited the silence seemed to stretch like elastic until she feared it might snap. She couldn't for the life of her imagine what he was finding so difficult about answering what had been a very simple question, yet she could see the battle waging inside his head.

She jumped as he finally moved, picked up his plate, carried it over to the sink, scraping the remnants into the disposal unit and rinsing it off before stowing it in the dishwasher.

'You're a very irritating woman, do you know that?' he said, slamming the door so that the rest of the crockery rattled.

That was a matter of opinion. She thought he more than matched her in that respect, but good manners—and her well-honed survival instincts—suggested it would be wiser not to say so. Instead she crossed the kitchen, picked up the kettle and began to fill it.

'A good cook, but irritating,' he continued, elaborating on his theme.

'One out of two isn't bad. I might have been irritating and a terrible cook.' She switched on the kettle and turned to face him. 'No redeeming features whatever.'

On that, apparently, he was not prepared to venture an opinion. Instead he asked, 'Is Maisie in bed?'

'It's nearly ten o'clock. Of course she's in bed.'

'There's no ''of course'' about it. She's usually up half the night, flouncing around, being spoilt by Sally's ridiculous friends.'

'Is she?' Why was she not surprised? 'Well, she's had a big day. She didn't even make the end of the story before she fell asleep.'

'Amazing.'

'You don't like her very much, do you?'

'Sally should stick to rescuing dumb animals,' he said, which didn't answer her question. But then you could often tell more from what people didn't say. And what he hadn't said would, she suspected, have filled volumes. 'She can abandon them up here once she's done the photo-call and there's no harm done.'

What...? Was he implying...?

'Maisie hasn't been abandoned,' she declared.

'No? What would you call it?'

'I'm sure that what happened today is nothing more than an unfortunate misunderstanding.' Not one that she'd have made, but she wasn't passing any judgements until she was in possession of all the facts. 'Actually, I did want to ask you something. Do you know if she keeps any clothes here? Outdoor play clothes? There was nothing in her room, but then it is something of a fairy grotto. Denim would undoubtedly spoil the illusion.'

'Undoubtedly. I'm afraid I can't help you. But she won't need them, since she isn't staying.'

Jacqui wasn't a violent woman, but if he'd been an inch or two smaller, she might just have seized his shoulders and shaken him. As it was, he'd probably laugh and his face might crack in two. Safer not to risk it. She'd have to start smaller. Try and tease out a smile...

She stopped. No point in wasting time worrying about 'smile' therapy; she would be more usefully employed in seizing the moment, reasoning with him. The kettle boiled just then, distracting her and by the time she'd poured water over a tea bag in a mug for herself, and made coffee for Harry Talbot, she'd thought better of it.

If she reasoned and failed, then he'd just end up more stubbornly fixed in the position he'd adopted. Every time he said 'she isn't staying' the words would became harder to retract.

And Maisie wanted to stay.

Better not give him the chance, she decided, dunking the tea bag.

Better to just wait until Vickie had spoken to Selina Talbot, at which point everything would doubtless resolve itself. And in the meantime she'd deal with the situation on the ground. One crisis at a time.

At least he seemed disinclined to rush off for once. She wouldn't get a better chance to talk to him. Nothing to threaten him—which was rather an odd thought under the circumstances; he was the ogre, not her—but just in the hope of finding common ground.

They hadn't, so far, had what could be described as a normal conversation.

'Does that chicken actually live in the kitchen?' she asked, saying the first thing that came into her head. *Normal?* 'Or is she sick?'

'The story is that one of the cats brought her in out of the rain when she was a chick and treated her as part of her litter.'

'Are you suggesting that she thinks she's a cat?'

'That's Aunt Kate's theory.' The look he gave her suggested otherwise.

'You're not buying that?'

'I haven't noticed any identity problem when the cockerel's preening his feathers, but if the choice was a basket in front of the stove or slumming it with the rest of the birds in the hen house, which would you choose?'

'That's a deeply cynical point of view.'

'And your answer is?'

'She's a smart hen.' Then, 'I'll bet the eggs confuse the heck out of the cats, though.'

There! She nearly had him with that one. He didn't actually smile, but there was definitely a giveaway crease at the side of his mouth. What he did do, was pick up the cafetière and pour himself a mug of coffee.

Classic distraction behaviour, she thought. She'd have done the same thing herself if she'd being trying to hide laughter. Or tears.

Maybe there was hope for him yet.

'Where were you going?' he asked, glancing sideways and catching her watching him.

'Nowhere,' she said, slightly flustered. She hadn't moved…

He turned and leaned back against the worktop, still looking at her. 'For your holiday?'

Oh, that. She'd forgotten all about Spain. Besides, it was warm enough in here to toast her skin. Not that he was crowding her. There was clear space between them, but the plush, wrap-around robe was much too warm.

And not nearly respectable enough.

It was too short, of course. They always were, but she'd never actually thought of her ankles as something she needed to cover up. But now her bare ankles seemed to suggest bare legs, which suggested all kinds of other possibilities.

And it felt much too tight.

While it was supposed to be her size, it had obviously been washed often and she had the unsettling feeling that somewhere down around her thighs it might be gaping open, just a bit.

She didn't dare look down.

To do so would simply draw attention to the fact. Not that he seemed interested in her legs.

On the contrary, his gaze seemed to be riveted on the deep vee where the wrap crossed over her breasts.

Not in any sense of the word leering. Just looking at her as if trying to remember something…

Which was crazy.

She was crazy.

She was, she reminded herself, a picture of modesty beneath this barely adequate robe.

When there was every likelihood that you'd have to turn out in the middle of the night, half-asleep, to tend to a disturbed child, it didn't take long to discover that smart nannies wore sensible PJs.

Not that it was a problem now, but she couldn't afford to toss out perfectly good nightwear and there was nothing in the least bit flimsy about the jersey sleep shorts and vest she was wearing. OK, this one just happened to be a vest top with shoestring straps—she'd seen a pack of three in a sale and treated herself for the holiday—but even so she'd have been wearing a lot less on a Spanish beach.

But then this wasn't a beach.

This was an isolated house with a man she didn't know. And he was staring at her cleavage.

Bad enough.

But her cleavage was responding...

# CHAPTER FIVE

'DO YOU want milk?' she asked. She didn't wait for his answer, but crossed to the fridge, taking her time about it, using the opportunity to wrap herself closer in the robe, pull the belt tighter while she had her back to him, before turning with the jug.

'No, thanks,' he said, when she offered it to him.

She had the feeling that he knew exactly what she'd done, but there was no sign of a self-congratulatory smirk. He just stared into his coffee as, discarding the tea bag, she splashed milk into her own mug.

'Isn't it rather late for black coffee?'

He didn't answer, just gave her a look that suggested she was treading a very fine line, but then he'd been doing variations of it since she'd arrived. It was, she suspected, supposed to have her running for cover. It reminded her of an unhappy child, testing to the limits her resolve to love her. Testing her promise to stay…

'Just my professional opinion,' she added.

'Keep it for Maisie, Mary Poppins.'

If he wanted her to duck for cover, he'd have to do better than that. Mary Poppins was, after all, 'practically perfect in every way'. One of the good guys.

'Lack of sleep can turn anyone into a grouch,' she said, not backing down, even though holding his gaze seemed to be having a detrimental effect on her knee joints. Turning them to mush as a small voice in her head whispered, 'Touch him. He needs someone to hold him…'

She cleared her throat to shut it up and said, 'But you're right, it's absolutely none of my business. Just don't blame me if you can't sleep.'

'Why not? I think we both know that you'll be the one keeping me awake—'

He paused, as if the image his words evoked had caught him by surprise and he'd forgotten what he was about to say. Time slowed and the air pressed against her, making her conscious of every inch of her skin as her mind filled with a picture of him in a dimly lit room, bare shoulders propped up against the pillow, arms behind his head, wide awake. Thinking about her.

It wasn't just her knees, but her entire body responded to this disturbing image with the heavy drag of sexual awareness, the ache of need. The swelling breasts, the taut, hard nipples almost painful against even the softest cloth. For so long immersed in a job that demanded everything of her, she'd forgotten how physical the demands of the body could be. How it could overpower the will, dominate all other thoughts...

'Like a thorn in your mattress,' she said, quickly, shattering the tension. Then, because she didn't want to dwell on his mattress, she quickly reverted to his earlier question and, answering it, said, 'Spain.'

'Spain?' Like her, he seemed to have come from somewhere deep inside himself. 'Oh, your holiday.' Then, 'On your own?'

She didn't think he'd have asked that question before and, while it would probably be wiser to just pick up her mug, say goodnight and retreat to the safety of her room, she'd be missing an opportunity to get to know him a little better.

For Maisie's sake, obviously.

So she sipped her tea, because her mouth seemed rather dry, and said, 'Does it matter?'

'If you were going with your boyfriend I'd imagine he'd be pretty fed up.'

'If I'd been going with a boyfriend, believe me, *I'd* be pretty fed up, but you needn't worry about some irate male turning up on your doorstep to add to the mayhem.'

He didn't look especially relieved, but then an irate male would probably have suited him very well. He was assuming he'd have an ally. She didn't bother to explain that what he'd have would be one more house guest while they sorted out the Maisie situation.

'At least there are plenty of flights to Spain.' Harry Talbot seemed determined to keep her focused on what was important in life. 'You'll only have missed a day.'

Well, she hadn't really thought he was interested in her well-being, had she? It was like the car. Getting it fixed was not thoughtfulness. Getting it fixed meant she had no excuse to stay.

'It's not that simple, I'm afraid. It was a cut-price last minute deal. If you don't show, tough luck.'

'You can't reschedule?'

*What planet was he on?*

'Don't bother your head about it. The agency will sort that out with your cousin. They've promised I won't be out of pocket.'

'I'm glad to hear it, but you won't get the money back for a couple of weeks, will you?'

She shrugged. 'It doesn't matter. I'm just doing temporary work at the moment so I can schedule my break to suit myself.' And she could think anywhere, after all. The sun would just be a distraction.

'That doesn't seem fair. If it would help I'll cover your losses and sort it out with Sally later.'

'Good grief, you *are* desperate to get rid of me.' A woman with self-esteem issues might have crumpled at this point, but she pulled a face in an attempt to suggest she found his persistence amusing. 'Paying to have my car fixed and now offering to sub me for a holiday.'

'I'm just doing my best to be reasonable.'

Reasonable!

Reasonable would be him saying—I'm sorry you've been put to so much trouble. Just make yourself at home while my useless family sorts itself out...

Or words to that effect.

'You really don't get it, do you?'

'Get what?'

She sipped her tea, then risked a glance at him over the rim of the mug. He looked, she thought, not so much uncaring as, well, a bit desperate, but she firmly quashed any feeling of guilt. She had done nothing to feel guilty about. He was the one behaving like a jerk.

'You must see that I can't go anywhere until I'm sure that Maisie is settled and safe.'

'Then I've got another suggestion, Miss Moore. Go to Spain and take Maisie with you.' He waited and, when he didn't get the ecstatic response he'd no doubt counted on, added, 'That way you'll get paid by the hour for lying in the sun.'

She laughed. 'You obviously have a very limited idea of what looking after a child entails.'

'I'll even pay for an upgrade.'

'I'm truly sorry,' she said. It was possible that she didn't sound entirely sincere, but then she wasn't. Despite what Maisie had told her, the man kept suckering her into thinking that he deserved some consid-

eration. He deserved absolutely nothing. 'Appealing as
your offer sounds, there are two very good reasons why
I can't accept. One, I'd need her legal guardian's written permission before I took Maisie out of the country—something that I'm sure even you'd agree is a
basic essential. It's not as if you know a single thing
about me.' And because, suddenly, she was really angry with him for being so completely lacking in family
feeling, so irresponsible, she said, 'Have you any idea
how much cute little girls fetch on the illegal-adoption
market?'

'I have a rather better idea of the cost than you, I
imagine.' Then, while she was still trying to get her
head around that one, 'And because I'm not as stupid
as you appear to believe, I called your agency this afternoon and the charming Mrs Campbell emailed me
your CV along with all manner of glowing testimoni-
als.'

'She did?'

'Why *did* you drop out of university in the middle
of your second year?'

'She did.'

She left it at that. He didn't want an answer to his
question; it had simply been a power play, a demon-
stration that he did indeed know all about her. While
she knew next to nothing about him. And what she did
know was all bad.

She wasn't having a very good day.

Little Princess, 2—Giant, 1…

'So,' he continued, 'now we've cleared up that small
problem and, assuming that, using the wonders of modern technology, Sally faxes her written permission to
your agency, what's your second objection?'

Everything, she thought, comes to she who waits. Time for Dumb Nanny to break her duck.

'Maisie wants to stay here,' she said. 'And my job—' she decided this might not be a good moment to tell him that she wasn't actually being paid for doing this '—is to keep her happy. Why don't you phone your new friend, Mrs Campbell, and ask her if she'd be prepared to take a bet on me doing just that?'

Despite the warm glow that putting a dent in his plans gave her, she anticipated a negative reaction to this challenge and, judging that this might be a good moment to leave, wasted no time about it.

'Goodnight, Mr Talbot,' she said, heading for the door. 'Sleep tight.' Actually, the 'sleep tight' was probably a mistake and it was just as well that she was carrying a mug of hot tea or she might have been tempted to make a run for it.

Not cool.

She'd managed to get in the last word and now she was leaving him—with dignity—to chew on it.

But as she walked across what seemed like a mile of quarry-tiled floor between her and the door, for every self-conscious inch of it aware of his gaze locked on her back, she didn't really expect to get away without some knife-edged parting shot.

'It's Harry,' he said, just as she made the safety of the door. 'Call me Harry.' Which was totally unexpected and then, when he had her full attention, added, 'I think we've traded sufficient insults to drop the formalities, don't you?'

Now that she'd had a chance to assess some of his finer points, Jacqui had to admit that she was tempted. No doubt about it, cleaned up, the man was six feet four inches of raw temptation. With a decent haircut and the serious application of razor to chin, she suspected he'd be dynamite.

Such a pity that he didn't have a heart to match his body.

'Are you offering to surrender, Mr Talbot?'

His jaw tightened, momentarily, and she had the uneasy impression that she was the one whose tongue was doing the cutting.

Impossible that a man of his stature, his character, could ever feel vulnerable, but she wished she'd kept her mouth shut for once and responded to his invitation with an encouraging smile, giving him a chance to tell her exactly what he was offering.

But then he lifted his massive shoulders in something that might have been a shrug, and said, 'No, Miss Moore. I'm simply suggesting a truce for the night.'

So that was all right, then. No damage done. He was just the same as ever.

She might be trapped on a fog-bound hill with the little princess and the big bad giant, but this wasn't a fairy tale. And while her coffee was good, it was going to take a lot more than one cup of the stuff to transform Harry Talbot into Prince Charming.

But then a kiss was the traditional cure…

'In that case,' she said, quickly, 'until the resumption of hostilities at dawn, goodnight. Harry.'

He looked, for a moment, as if he was about to respond and she waited, her hand on the edge of the door, hoping for some indication that he was relenting. Offering something more.

But all he said was, 'Goodnight, Jacqui.'

After that, she had no choice but to close the door and walk away, but she climbed the stairs to the second floor with a hollow feeling of regret. There was nothing that she could put her finger on, just the niggling certainty that she'd come close to something important but had been too busy defending her own position to see it properly.

She looked in on Maisie, straightened her tumbled covers, watched her for a while before going to her own room.

Harry did not move for a long time. The coffee cooled in his mug. In the pot. And still he waited for the air to still, settle, return to the way it had been until Jacqui Moore had stirred everything up.

After a while, a cat stretched and moved to the door, a dark shadow heading out for the night's hunt. The scruffy hound rose on long legs and padded across to nose at his hand, politely suggesting it was time for a walk.

The animals seemed unaware of the eddies created by her presence still spinning through the air, disturbing the atmosphere, disturbing the emptiness, disturbing him.

He moved swiftly, rounded up the rest of the dogs, not stopping to put on the coat he grabbed from the peg as he set off across the hill. The old Labradors turned back after a while, but the hound stayed with him as he covered the miles in his determination to dislodge her from his mind. From his heart.

Jacqui left Maisie deciding between pink taffeta and yellow silk and went downstairs determined to find something rather more practical for her to wear.

She glanced in the small office, but there was no sign of Harry Talbot. No sign that he'd even been in the room, since the bag of mail she'd left on the desk was exactly how she'd left it.

She had better luck in the kitchen, which was occupied by a motherly woman busy emptying the dishwasher.

'Are you Susan?' she asked, cheered by the sight of a possible ally. 'I'm Jacqui. Maisie's nanny. Temporarily.' There seemed little point in confusing matters by trying to explain exactly what the situation was. 'Did Mr Talbot explain about the misunderstanding?'

'Mr Harry? No. But then I stay out of his way as much as I can,' she said, wiping her hands on her apron. 'I only come up here every day because the missus refused to go until I promised her I'd keep an eye on everything. Make sure he's got something to eat.' Then, with a shrug, 'Of course, I did hear that someone turned up with Miss Maisie yesterday afternoon.'

Since it was undoubtedly the hot item of gossip in the village shop, Jacqui wasn't exactly surprised to hear that. They were, no doubt, panting for an update from their woman on the inside.

'I was expecting to find Mrs Talbot here. The plan was for Maisie to stay with her while her mother's away.'

'Really? It's news to me. She went to New Zealand, you know. To stay with her sister.'

'Mr Talbot told me she was away.'

'Paid for everything, he did. She went first class.'

'That was generous of him.'

'Possibly,' she said, not committing herself one way or the other, although what doubt there could be, escaped Jacqui.

'She didn't say anything about Maisie coming to stay?'

'Well, no. Miss Sally doesn't make arrangements that far ahead.'

Jacqui frowned. Far ahead? 'When did Mrs Talbot go to New Zealand?'

'Last November.'

'But that's five months ago.'

'That's right. She took her time. Went by boat for part of the way. She got there in time for Christmas though.'

'Oh.'

'No point going all that way for five minutes, is there?'

'Er—no. Is she due back soon?'

'Not that I heard. In her last letter she said that as long as Mr Harry is happy to stay and keep an eye on things, she'll stay on for a bit.'

'And Mr Ha...Mr Talbot's happy, is he?'

'Well, I wouldn't say happy, exactly, but he's in no hurry to leave. It's the nearest thing he's got to a home.'

It was?

She bit back the question hovering on her lips. One step further down that path would be gossip.

'I don't understand why Miss Talbot sent Maisie here. She must have known her mother wasn't here to look after her.'

'Lives in a world of her own, that one. Always has.'

'Even so, it's hard to see how anyone could have made such a mistake,' she prompted, putting on the kettle. 'Can I make you a cup of tea?'

'Not now, thank you. I'm just going to give the chickens a bit of do. But I'll have one when I come

back if you like. It's perishing out there this morning.'
She gave Jacqui a look that suggested she was two
jumpers and a pair of long johns short of dressed and
headed for the door.

Disappointed—she didn't approve of *gossip*, but she
had been hoping for a cosy chat around the teapot and
some answers to any number of questions that had kept
her awake half the night—she said, 'No problem.'
Then, 'Before you disappear, could I ask you something?'

'You can ask,' she replied, warily. 'I can't promise
you an answer.'

'It's just that Maisie hasn't brought any outdoor
clothes with her. There are none in her room and Mr
Talbot doesn't seem to know whether she keeps spares
here.'

'Well, why would he?'

Jacqui was beginning to understand why a thwarted
two-year-old might throw a tantrum. It was the same
inability to communicate. Obviously there was an answer out there...she just couldn't seem to frame the
right question.

Old enough to know that throwing herself on the
floor and drumming her heels—no matter how tempting—was not a constructive response to frustration, she
tried again.

'Actually, I don't know. I don't know anything.'

Maybe humility was the answer, because Susan said,
'Well, he's always off gallivanting to some foreign
place or other, isn't he? Never a word for months, years
even, then he just turns up.'

Just her luck that their visits happened to coincide...
Much as she'd have liked to pursue this further,

Susan was already heading for the mud room. 'Do *you* know?' she asked, a touch desperately.

The woman thought about it for a minute, then shook her head, reinforcing the message with a simple, 'No.'

Blunt, but at least direct. 'Maybe I could look around and check for myself,' she suggested. 'Where would be a good place to start?'

'I told you, she doesn't keep any clothes here.' With that she reached into the mud room and unhooked a coat. 'Her last nanny always packed everything she needed.' The criticism was unspoken, but it was scarcely veiled.

'I didn't have that luxury. I'm having to manage with what I was given. Pink taffeta and wellington boots it's going to have to be.'

'I suppose you could take a look in the old nursery,' Susan said, relenting as she took a headscarf from her pinafore pocket. 'You might find something of Miss Sally's in there. It's up the stairs, and...' she thought for a moment '...five doors down.'

'Thank you, Susan.' She smiled. 'I expect you'll be ready for a bacon sandwich when you've sorted the hens. To go with your tea.'

The woman grinned. 'Go on, then. If you insist. I'll be about half an hour.'

Which gave her plenty of time to scout the 'old nursery'.

She climbed the first flight of stairs and, as instructed, turned right through an arch and immediately found herself in a wide corridor, lit on one side by a series of windows that must have offered a fine view when it wasn't obscured by ground-level cloud.

The polished floor was bisected by a Turkey runner and the inner wall furnished with antique chests and some fine pictures, serving to remind her that, despite her first impressions, this was a substantial house. Slightly shabby on the outside, maybe, but very much what had once been called a 'gentleman's residence'.

Shame about the gentleman in residence she thought, counting the doors until she came to the fifth. It was near the top of a fine flight of stairs. The premier position in the house and scarcely where she'd have expected to find the nursery, but she shrugged and, opening the door, walked in. Since it was early and the hill fog, still clinging close to the house, made the rooms dark, she reached for the light switch.

An ornate overhead light fitting sprang into life and she immediately realised that she'd been right. This wasn't a nursery, but the master bedroom and furnished in high style by the 'gentleman' whose residence this had been some time back in the Regency. Elegant, expensive and with an impressive four-poster bed dominating the room.

She turned, her intention to immediately withdraw. And found herself face to face with Harry Talbot, standing in front of a chest of drawers, apparently looking for underwear.

Bad enough that she'd walked into his room without even knocking, but then there was the small fact that he'd just stepped out of the shower and was naked but for a towel slung carelessly about his hips.

As he spun to face her it lost its battle with gravity.

He made no move to retrieve it and, despite opening her mouth with every intention of apologising for having blundered into his room, she found herself quite unable to speak.

He was beautiful.

Lean to the bone, hard, sculptured, his was the kind

of body artists loved for their life classes. Even his hair, thick and heavy, had sprung into thick curls down which droplets of water ran in a slow, sensuous trickle. She watched one fall onto his shoulder, run down his chest until it became part of him.

He represented the perfection of Michelangelo's *David*.

Which made the scars lacerating his back, scars which he hadn't moved quickly enough to hide from her, all the more terrible.

Without thinking, she reached out, as if to touch him, take the pain into her own body. Before her fingers made contact, he seized her wrist and in one swift, savage movement thrust her out of the room.

Then he said, 'Stay there. Don't move.' He didn't wait to see if she obeyed him, but shut the door in her face.

She didn't need him to tell her to stay put.

While all her instincts were to run, hide, her legs were beyond movement. Her entire body was trembling and she covered her mouth with her hand as if to stop herself from screaming.

What had happened to him? The ridges of scar tissue where his flesh had been ripped and torn were like nothing she had ever seen. Nothing she ever wanted to see again.

She groaned and leaned against the door arch, almost falling in on him as he opened the door, this time wrapped in a thick towelling robe.

'Are you all right?' he asked, catching her, holding her arms so tightly to keep her at a distance that his fingers dug into her flesh. She didn't complain. She didn't for one moment believe it was intentional.

She didn't ask what he meant, either. She just nodded and he relaxed his grip sufficiently for her circulation to be restored. But he didn't let go.

Maybe, she thought, close enough now to see that the beginnings of a beard disguised just how gaunt he looked—as if he hadn't slept in a long time—he's the one who needs a prop.

'So what did you want that couldn't wait? Has Sally been in touch?'

So cool. So matter-of-fact. So do-not-even-think-about-mentioning-what-you-saw. But for the painful pressure points in her arms, she might actually have been fooled.

'No. It's too early to call the agency…' Then, because he wasn't interested in what she hadn't done, just what the devil she was doing bursting into his room unannounced, she took a rather shaky breath and did her best to match his tone as she continued, 'I wasn't actually looking for you. I was looking for the old nursery. S-Susan said there might be something more suitable for Maisie to wear. Up the s-stairs, fifth door along, she said…'

As if it mattered what Susan had said. Or whether Maisie played in the stables wearing a party frock, as long as she was warm enough. She had to know…

'Harry—'

'She assumed you'd be coming up the front stairs,' he said, cutting her off before she could ask the question. 'It's this way.' And he walked her back down the corridor, his hand gripping her firmly beneath her elbow as if to stop her bolting, or fainting, or saying one word about what she'd seen. 'Help yourself,' he said, opening a door. Then turned abruptly and walked away.

'Harry!'

He stopped at the entrance to his room, not looking at her. 'Don't ask,' he warned.

For a moment neither of them moved, neither of them spoke. Then, apparently satisfied that he'd made his point, he stepped inside and closed the door.

## CHAPTER SIX

MAISIE, having finally settled on pink taffeta, was not impressed with the alternatives Jacqui had found.

'They smell,' she said, wrinkling her nose in disgust.

'Only because they haven't been worn in a long time. I'm not asking you to put them on until they've been washed. I just want to make sure they fit.'

'They won't.'

'Probably not,' she agreed. 'I think your mother must have been taller than you.'

'No, she wasn't. I'm exactly the same height as she was, she told me.'

Pride...so predictable.

'Oh, well, these were hers, so that's all right.'

'Oh, *please*.' Maisie, quickly recovering from her mistake, picked up a sweatshirt featuring a cartoon character and held it at arm's length. 'My mother wouldn't ever have been seen *dead* wearing something like this.'

Having anticipated this reaction, Jacqui produced a photograph that she'd found pinned to a display board in the nursery. It was curling at the edges, very faded and had doubtless been pinned up because of the puppy a very young Selina Talbot was cuddling, rather than for any aesthetic reason.

Or maybe it was because, behind her, an older, taller, protective presence, stood her big cousin, Harry.

The reason didn't matter. What mattered was that she was wearing that sweatshirt.

'Why would she keep a dumb sweatshirt?' Maisie demanded, giving her back the picture, not thrilled to be proved wrong.

'Haven't you ever kept a favourite dress, even when it doesn't fit you any more,' she asked, 'just to remember how you felt when you wore it?'

Maisie shrugged. 'I s'pose.' Then, 'Is that Harry with my mother?'

She looked at the photograph again and then offered it back to the child. 'Why don't you ask him?'

'No,' she said, fiddling with a button rather than take it. 'It's him.'

'Unless he's got a twin brother,' she agreed.

On second thoughts, there was no question in her mind why Selina had kept the photograph where she could see it. The man might have some serious flaws, but the boy had been built for hero-worship. And his hand on her shoulder would have made the sweatshirt special, too.

Probably.

Or maybe that was emotional transference...

'OK, it's miserable outside at the moment so you can't go out to play, but in the meantime I'll put this through the wash and then maybe, if the cloud lifts this afternoon, I could take a photograph of you wearing it.'

No response.

'With one of the puppies? You could give them both to your mother when she comes home. I'm sure she'd like that.'

'Only if Harry will be in it, too,' Maisie insisted, aware that she'd painted herself into a corner, but giving it one last shot. 'So that it's exactly the same.'

'That's a lovely idea,' she said. Although whether

Harry Talbot would think so was another matter entirely.

'Will you ask him for me?'

There was a whole world of want—need—in those few words and she said, 'Yes, sweetheart. Of course I'll ask him.'

'First. Before I put *that* on.'

She should have seen that coming.

Maisie was little, but she was bright and she knew when she was being sold a pup—in every sense of the word.

Jacqui was saved any immediate challenge to her negotiating skills, since—unsurprisingly—Harry wasn't hanging around waiting for a chat. Once breakfast was over she left Maisie 'helping' Susan with some baking and went to call Vickie.

As she opened the office door, Harry looked up from the pile of post he'd tipped out of the carrier bag, his eyes so fierce that she took a step back.

'I'm sorry. I didn't mean to disturb you.'

'Your presence in the house disturbs the very air,' he declared. Then, after what might have been a deep breath, or possibly a ten-count while he regained his composure, 'I accept, however, that there's nothing you can do about it so will you please stop tiptoeing around me?'

'It would help if you didn't look as if you were offended by the mere sight of me,' she pointed out.

'I'm not...' he began irritably, then stopped, perhaps unwilling to perjure himself and dismissing the matter with a gesture that suggested she was being over-sensitive. Then did what any man who knew he was wrong would do; went on the attack. 'Did you leave this pile of garbage here?'

'If you're referring to the mail, then yes. The woman running the village shop asked me to bring it up. When I stopped for directions.'

'Then when you leave I suggest you give it back to her and tell her—'

'I've got a better idea, Mr Talbot,' she said, fed up with being the butt of his ill-humour. Whatever trauma he'd suffered, she wasn't to blame. 'Why don't you...' breathe, Jacqui, breathe '...tell her yourself?' Then, because she wasn't averse to a little subject changing when she'd overstepped her own aggression threshold, 'Have you heard from your cousin?'

He shook his head. 'No joy from your agency, I suppose?'

'I was just about to ring them.'

'Help yourself.'

He pushed the telephone towards her and she lifted the receiver, then jiggled the button a couple of times. 'There's no dial tone.'

He took it from her and listened as if he didn't believe she knew her dialling tone from her elbow. The man, she thought, had a very underdeveloped sense of self-preservation.

'Am I mistaken?' she asked, with deceptive sweetness.

It was, of course, possible that his rudeness was a shield against unwanted pity.

If so, it was working.

He muttered something beneath his breath. She didn't ask him to repeat it; she didn't think it was anything she was meant—or would want—to hear.

NO POSTAGE
NECESSARY
IF MAILED
IN THE
UNITED STATES

**BUSINESS REPLY MAIL**

FIRST-CLASS MAIL    PERMIT NO. 717-003    BUFFALO, NY

POSTAGE WILL BE PAID BY ADDRESSEE

HARLEQUIN READER SERVICE
3010 WALDEN AVE
PO BOX 1867
BUFFALO NY 14240-9952

# Get FREE BOOKS and a FREE GIFT when you play the...

# LAS VEGAS
### GAME

*Just scratch off the gold box with a coin. Then check below to see the gifts you get!*

**YES!** I have scratched off the gold box. Please send me my 2 **FREE BOOKS** and **gift for which I qualify.** I understand that I am under no obligation to purchase any books as explained on the back of this card.

▼ DETACH AND MAIL CARD TODAY! ▼

386 HDL D7YM            186 HDL D7ZN

| | | | | | | | | | | | | |
|---|---|---|---|---|---|---|---|---|---|---|---|---|

FIRST NAME                    LAST NAME

ADDRESS

APT.#        CITY

STATE/PROV.        ZIP/POSTAL CODE

(H-R-12/05)

| 7 | 7 | 7 | Worth TWO FREE BOOKS plus a BONUS Mystery Gift! |
| 🍒 | 🍒 | 🍒 | Worth TWO FREE BOOKS! |
| 🔔 | 🔔 | ♣ | TRY AGAIN! |

www.eHarlequin.com

'It happens all the time up here,' he went on. 'Just as well you've got a cellphone.'

'I'll report the fault, shall I?'

'If you must.'

She bit back her first thought, which was that, no, actually, she was quite happy to leave him without contact with the outside world and that she was sure the outside world would thank her.

No point in going out of her way to aggravate the man when she was doing such a good job of it without any effort at all, especially as she had a favour to ask him. For Maisie.

But not yet.

Phone call first.

If the news was good, he'd be in a better mood.

That was the theory, anyway. There was only one problem with it; she couldn't find her cellphone.

Leaving Harry alone in his office, she checked her pocket, which was where her phone lived during the day. Then checked the bedside table, which was where it usually spent the night.

But yesterday hadn't been usual in any sense of the word: witness the silver chain lying where her phone should be. She picked it up and fastened it around her wrist—just for safety—then checked beneath the bed in case it had fallen on the floor, before retracing all her moves without any luck.

It wasn't in the kitchen either, and Maisie, enveloped in a huge apron and with smears of flour across her cheeks, just looked blank when asked if she'd seen it.

The office was the only place left and, since it was the last place she actually remembered having it, she had no choice but to enter the lion's den for the second time that morning. This time she took the precaution of tapping on the door before opening it.

Harry looked up. 'Well?'

'Not so's you'd notice,' she said. 'I can't find my phone. If it isn't in here I don't know where else to look.'

'I didn't see it, but then I wasn't looking.' He indicated the mail spread across the desk—most of it of the junk variety and still apparently untouched. 'Dig in. You might find anything under this lot.'

She picked up a handful of the stuff and went through it tossing most of it into the waste basket unopened—having brought it to the house, it was the least she could do—leaving personal mail and bills in separate piles to one side. When she looked up, she realised that he was watching her.

'What?'

He shook his head. 'Carry on, you're doing a fine job.'

'It's good to know I'm useful for something, even if it is only getting rid of the rubbish.' But she began to feel self-conscious as he continued to watch her. 'You can put a block on most of this stuff, you know. It's almost your duty, in fact. One phone call to save the planet…' Then, as she binned the last of the circulars, straightened the papers on the desk, 'All you need is a phone. It's not on the desk, is it?' Then, beginning to feel a touch desperate, 'This is ridiculous. It's got to be here somewhere. Would you mind standing up?'

She dug around the back and sides of a chair warmed by his body, totally aware that the taut backside and thighs just inches from her face were the source of that heat.

'It's not here,' she said, backing off.

'Maybe it fell on the floor.'

She'd already dropped to her knees before she realised that instead of standing aside and leaving her to it, he'd done the same. Looking up, expecting to be confronted by nothing more dangerous than his knees, she found herself looking straight into his eyes.

The cool thing would have been to smile, and carry on looking. She didn't feel cool. This close, his tawny eyes generated enough heat to sear her entire body and she reared back, crashing against the edge of the desk and falling back to her knees with a whimper of pain.

The next thing she knew she was sitting in his chair and he was crouched in front of her, looking into her eyes. 'Jacqui?'

'It's OK...' she said, making a move to rise. 'I'm OK.'

His hand on her shoulder kept her in the chair. 'Don't move for a minute. You took quite a knock.'

'No, really.' But her head felt as if it had just exploded and her legs were kitten-weak. Despite her protest, she stayed where she was. 'I'll be all right in a moment.'

'Look at me.' Oh, right. That was what had caused the trouble in the first place... 'How many fingers am I holding up?'

Having satisfied himself that she wasn't seeing double, he stood up and began to gently part her hair, just above her forehead, taking a closer look at the damage.

'Excuse me?' she said, but nowhere near as in-your-face what-the-heck-do-you-think-you're-doing as she'd intended. 'Are you a doctor?'

'Yes, and I can tell you that the prognosis is a headache and a lump the size of an egg.'

'I could have told *you* that...' Wince. Oooch. Too much talking... 'Are you really a doctor?'

'I'm somewhat out of practice,' he admitted, 'but I think I can handle a minor bump on the head.'

'Minor!' she exclaimed.

'See? You're almost back to normal. I'll go and get an ice-pack.'

'There's no need.'

'You're disputing my diagnosis? Are you a doctor, too?'

'Sarcasm is so unattractive.' Then, 'Besides, you've read my CV. You know exactly what I am.'

'I've got a fair idea, although I'd still like to know why you dropped out of your nursing course at university.' She took a breath to speak but he raised a warning finger that didn't quite touch her lips. 'Save it. Keep quiet and don't move. I'll be right back.'

'I was just going to tell you to mind your own business,' she muttered rebelliously, but only after he'd left the room.

Obviously he knew what he was talking about when he'd advised her to keep quiet, because she wished she'd obeyed him.

'Susan is making you a cup of tea,' he said, returning a minute or two later with crushed ice wrapped in a cloth. He laid it gently against her forehead and said, 'How's that?'

'Cold?' she offered. Then, because that sounded ungrateful, 'Wonderfully cold.' It was certainly a lot better than the thought of tea, the very idea of which made her feel sick. She didn't tell him that; Dr Harry Talbot would be diagnosing concussion and whisking her off to hospital before she could say Jack Robinson and wouldn't that make him a happy bunny...? 'Thank you,' she added, reaching up to take over the job of holding the ice-pack in place, her fingers getting entangled in his as they changed over.

'What's Maisie doing?' she asked, more as a distraction than out of any deep concern.

'Being Maisie.'

Weirdly, she understood exactly what he meant, but, feeling guilty as well as stupid, she said, 'Damn it! What have I done with my phone? I was sure I'd put it in my pocket.'

'Maybe it's fallen out somewhere. You'll find it when it rings.'

'But I want it *now*!' Then, blushing—that sounded sooo like Maisie at her very worst— 'Sorry... I just need to know what's happening. Maisie shouldn't be left out on a limb like this.'

'I thought you said she wanted to stay.'

'That's not the point.' Then, leaning her elbows on the desk, both hands clutching the ice-pack as she rested her head against it and trying to think through the pain... 'But you're right. She seems happy enough.'

'But of course you want to get on with your own life.'

'I didn't say that.' She looked up at him from under her hands. 'Did I say that?'

'No.' He looked as if he was going to say something but clearly changed his mind. Then, after a moment, 'Did you find her anything more practical to wear in the meantime?'

'Yes. And then again no.'

'Well, that's clear.' He doubled up opposite her as if to check that her eyes weren't glazing over.

'I found her some stuff,' she said, rousing herself,

'but she really doesn't see herself as a sweatshirt and jeans girl.'

'She can't spend her entire life in party dresses,' he objected, not moving. 'She must have some ordinary clothes.'

'Your confidence does you credit. But yes, I suppose you're right. There's obviously been some kind of a slip-up on the packing front. Fortunately I found this.' She dug around in her shirt pocket and fished out the photograph she'd found. Her fingers were wet and she wiped it on her sleeve before handing it to him. 'It's her mother wearing the same stuff.'

He stared at it for a moment, then returned it to her, without comment. 'Did it do the trick?'

'Would you exchange pink taffeta frills for denim bib overalls without a fuss?'

'Fortunately, I've never had to make that choice.'

Was that a smile? Just the tiniest hint of one?

Encouraged, she said, 'Actually, I had a bit of a brainwave and suggested I take a photograph of her exactly like this one. That seemed to do the trick.'

'So what's the problem? You need a camera? There's got to be one around here somewhere.'

'Thanks, but I have a camera. I was going on holiday,' she reminded him.

'Then why is she still in the pink frilly thing? I mean, there's no shortage of puppies.'

'No. But it's not just the puppy.' She wasn't likely to have his undivided attention again any time soon. Best not waste it. 'You were in the original photograph and she wants one *exactly* like it.' Then, because she didn't want him to say no without giving it some thought, she quickly added, 'There's no rush. The clothes are in the wash and it's not exactly fit to take photographs out there this morning.' Even if she could see straight. 'In the meantime I'd better go and have another look for my phone.'

'Jacqui…'

She made an effort to stand, but her knees didn't feel quite up to it. It was nothing to do with the way he'd said her name. Very softly, not as if he wanted to make sure she was listening, but just because he wanted to say it…

'I'm sorry.'

Her mistake.

'What for?' There were so many things to choose from… 'It wasn't your fault I banged my head.'

'About your holiday.'

Oh, that…

'I promise I won't say another word about it if you'll let Maisie have her photograph.'

'You provide the sun—' he didn't exactly growl, the embryo smile had gone but he didn't seem bothered by her blatant attempt at a little emotional blackmail '—and I'll turn up for the photo call.'

Which implied that he knew something about the prevailing weather conditions at Hill Tops that she didn't.

It didn't matter. He'd promised. And the sun had to shine eventually, if she stuck around for long enough— it had been shining in that old photograph she'd found, hadn't it?—which was why, instead of responding with something snippy like 'you've got a deal', she smiled—a real smile this time—and said, 'Thank you.' Then, rather more weakly, 'Now we've sorted that out, is there any chance of a couple of aspirin?'

'Only if you'll lie down for an hour and give them a chance to do their job.'

'Are you sending me to bed?'

No, no, stupid thing to say. The way she felt at that moment, he'd have to carry her and she didn't think that lying against his chest listening to his heart being put through its paces—she wasn't stick-thin like his glamorous cousin—would do her condition any good at all.

'What about Maisie?' she demanded, in an attempt to shift that image from her brain.

'Susan will take care of her.'

'She's got other things to do. Chickens, house-work…'

'That isn't your problem.'

OK, so she'd been hoping he might have a complete change of heart and volunteer to take care of Maisie himself, but her head hurt too much to worry about it.

'All right. But there's no way I'm going to bed. You'll have to ask those dogs to budge up and let me share their sofa.'

'I could, of course, insist that you go to the local A&E for an X-ray, since you're obviously not in your right mind.' Then, taking pity on her, 'Come on. You can put your feet up in the library.'

'The library? You mean you're letting me back into the posh bit of the house? After this morning?'

She blinked. Had she really said that? The crack to her skull must have been harder than she'd thought.

He clamped his jaw down hard, presumably because it was against medical ethics to yell at someone in pain. Demand that they shut up.

She actually saw the slow breath he took, although if he counted to ten he did it mentally, before he said, 'I think "posh" might be stretching it a bit, but at least you won't get covered in dog hairs.'

She thought she should probably say something, but couldn't think of anything sensible, so left it and he put a hand beneath her elbow, eased her to her feet.

'Can you walk?'

'Of course I can walk,' she said, doing her best to ignore the fact that the room was spinning and clutching the ice-pack to her head. 'I'm not an invalid.'

'No, just a pain in the backside. Don't you ever give your mouth a rest?'

'Of course I...' She stopped. 'That was a trick question, wasn't it?'

He didn't answer, possibly to demonstrate that one of them had some control over their mouth, although if she had been a betting woman she might have had a mild flutter on the chance that it was because he was trying not to laugh. Definitely trying not to laugh. Almost definitely.

And, OK, doing a pretty good job of it.

She had a quick glimpse of panelled hall, the bottom of the substantial oak staircase that led to his bedroom and then she was in a room that had the perfect air of shabby comfort only attained through generations of occupation by the same family.

Velvet curtains that had once been green, but which now, except in the deepest folds, had faded to a silvery grey. A richly patterned Persian rug, worn practically threadbare. A huge Knole sofa standing four-square to a handsome fireplace which was laid with logs and only needed a match to send the reflection of flames flickering off the bookshelves that lined the walls.

Not a bit like the bare stone interior of the horrible giant's house in her childhood story book.

First impressions could be so wrong...

Harry crossed to the hearth and hunkered down to

put a match to the fire, although the room wasn't cold. She perched on the edge of the sofa as he coaxed the fire to life, watching his deft movements, quick reaction as a log fell into the hearth, his broad back. And forgot her own pain as her stomach wrenched in empathy for pain she could not even imagine. And she closed her eyes.

'Jacqui?' She jerked them open. 'Are you OK?'

'Yes,' she said, but without conviction.

'You look a bit pale. Do you feel sick?'

She did, but not as a result of the bang on the head. 'I'm fine, really.'

He continued to look at her for a moment, before turning back to the fire. When he was sure it had caught, he placed a guard in front of it.

'Shall I take that?'

She looked down at the ice-pack, which was beginning to melt into her lap. 'None of this is necessary,' she protested. 'I should be—'

'What?'

Looking for her phone. Chasing Vickie to find out what was happening. But then, as Harry had pointed out, Maisie was happy enough. This was what she'd wanted. So why was she getting her knickers in a twist, instead of doing as she was told, lying back and letting everything work itself out?

'Nothing,' she said.

'Right answer.'

And this time the crease at the corner of his mouth was deep enough to qualify as a smile. Lopsided maybe. A trifle wry, even. But a heart-stopping improvement on the alternative.

She could live with 'wry'.

'Now all you have to do is put your feet up and I'll go and get some aspirin.'

And to prevent any further argument, he bent, picked her feet up in one hand, pulled off her shoes and placed them on the sofa.

# CHAPTER SEVEN

WHEN Harry returned a couple of minutes later with aspirin and a blanket, Jacqui was asleep. He watched her for a while. Her colour had returned and her breathing was good, but there were dark smudges beneath her eyes that had nothing to do with the crack on the head.

He'd noticed them last night when she'd come down—minus the make-up she'd used to conceal them—to make herself a drink. Jacqui Moore, he suspected, hadn't been sleeping properly for some time. Something he knew all about.

No doubt there was a man at the bottom of it. Why else would she be going on holiday on her own?

He left the painkillers on the sofa table and, as gently as he could, covered her with the blanket.

'How is she?'

He turned as Susan came in with tea.

'She's dropped off. Best thing for her.'

'She shouldn't be left. My sister's boy fell out of a tree—'

'Yes, thank you, Susan. I'll stay and keep an eye on her. Just leave the tray.'

'Right. Well, I'm off upstairs to do the bedrooms if you want me.'

'Take Maisie with you. I don't want her coming in here disturbing Jacqui.'

Susan made a sound that only women beyond a certain age could manage. She 'humphed'. It said more clearly than words that she knew exactly what he didn't want. Maisie disturbing *him*. Then she said, 'She should be at school, playing with children her own age.'

'Save the lecture for Sally when she turns up.'

'I won't hold my breath.' Then, 'I'm sure Mrs Jackson, the head teacher, would be happy to take her until the end of term.'

'No doubt, but she's not staying.' He gave the final three words equal weight, hoping that someone would finally get the message.

'If you say so.' She put down the tray. 'Well, I can't stand about here gossiping. If you need anything you know where I am.'

'Will you keep an eye out for Jacqui's cellphone? It wasn't in the office so she must have dropped it upstairs somewhere.'

'I'll do that.'

As she turned to leave they both saw Maisie, half-hidden by the open door, apparently afraid to venture closer.

'Is she dead?' she whispered. 'Did I kill her?'

'You?' Susan exclaimed. 'Why on earth would you think something—?'

He crossed swiftly to the door, bundling them both out. 'She bumped her head on the desk, Maisie. It had nothing to do with you,' he said, putting a stop to the discussion.

'But she was looking—'

'She'll be fine. She just needs peace and quiet for an hour, that's all. Go along with Susan, now.'

'I'd rather go to school.'

*Thank you, Susan...*

'Can I? In the village? Now? Pleeease...'

She was unusually twittery. He might even have said anxious...

'I don't think so. Maybe,' he added, cruelly, 'if your mother had packed something sensible for you to wear—'

'Don't blame her! It wasn't her fault! I did it. I just wanted to look pretty so you'd like me!'

Then, as if horrified by what she had said, she turned and ran off.

Susan just looked at him. 'You know, Mr Harry, it's not my place to say so, but in my opinion that child needs a little order in her life.'

'You're right, Susan,' he said. 'It isn't your place to say so.'

She sniffed, leaving him in no doubt what she was thinking, and went after Maisie.

The hound had taken advantage of Susan's arrival to slip into the library and was lying as flat as possible in front of the fire, hoping not to be noticed.

He added another log and then turned to make sure Jacqui hadn't been disturbed. She was curled up on her side, her cheek resting on her hands, a strand of silky hair slipping across her forehead.

He eased a finger beneath it, lifting it carefully out of her face. And that was when he noticed the silver chain about her wrist. Really noticed it.

He'd been aware of a bracelet sliding down her arm when she was holding the ice-pack.

What he saw now was the single charm, a silver heart. It was engraved with a message, tiny words that he knew were none of his business, but as he moved back the angle of the light changed and the words seemed to leap out at him—'...forget and smile...'

He knew it from somewhere and he searched the

shelves for a dictionary of quotations, finally found the couplet.

And he felt…something.

He'd shut out every emotion, every feeling for so long that he couldn't say what it was. Only that it hurt. That if he didn't blot it out the pain would become unbearable.

But then he'd recognised the danger the moment she'd jammed her foot in his door and refused to be shut out. He'd tried, but unlike most people, she seemed immune to his rudeness. It was almost, he thought, as if she understood what he was doing.

Ridiculous, of course. She didn't know him or anything about him.

Yet she'd found a way into his house, into his life and he was afraid that she wouldn't be content until she'd prised open the armour plating he'd donned to keep out the prurient, the intrusive, those seekers after the second-hand shiver of horror who'd demand every last detail if he weakened, let down the barrier…

Right now that seemed the least of his worries. The outside world he could keep at bay. It was what was locked up inside him that he couldn't face.

Reeling away from the sofa, he took a biography from the shelves and settled into an armchair. Reading, watching. Watching…

Jacqui stirred. Winced as her forehead came in contact with the side of the sofa. Remembered. And risked opening her eyes.

The logs had burned down to a hot, almost translucent glow. The shaggy hound, who she was sure had no business in the library, was stretched out in blissful slumber in front of it. She gingerly felt for the damage to her scalp. It was tender, although the prophesied lump was barely noticeable, and, having decided that she'd survive, she eased herself carefully upright, taking care not to make any sudden moves. And that was when she saw that it was not just the dog who'd kept her company.

Harry Talbot was sitting in a high-backed armchair set to one side of the hearth. He'd been reading, but the book had fallen to the floor and he was fast asleep.

Most people—and she included herself in that 'most'—looked slightly undefined in sleep; the curve of cheek and chin sagging a little as flesh succumbed to gravity. But there was no softness in Harry's pared-to-the-bone features.

The difference was not in the letting go of muscle tone, but the absence of tension.

The strain had gone from his face and the change was such that she finally understood that it wasn't her, or Maisie, he was battling to keep out with his rudeness. It was the entire world.

She didn't disturb him, but instead tucked up her feet and, easing up the down-soft cushion that had been pillowed beneath her, curled up against the high side of the sofa.

The dog raised his head hopefully, but she put a finger to her lips and whispered, 'Lie down.'

Maybe he understood, or maybe he was smart enough to realise that, since she was staying put, he had nothing to gain—and a warm place in front of the fire to lose—if he moved and disturbed the sleeping man. But he dropped his chin back onto his paws, rolled his eyes up at Harry and sighed.

Like Maisie, he was another soul yearning for a kind word, a tender touch from the object of adoration.

The thought took her somewhat by surprise. Why would Maisie yearn for attention from Harry? If he really had a problem with her adoption? Had there been something shady about that? He'd implied he knew about such things.

Yet that awkward, slightly aggressive way Maisie talked about him, acted around him, bore all the hallmarks of an unspoken need to be noticed, loved.

'Penny for them?'

She jumped, dragged out of her thoughts by Harry's voice.

'Sorry,' he said. 'I didn't mean to startle you. How's the head?'

'OK. A bit tender where I caught the corner of the desk, but actually—' she smiled, although the nod that went with it might have been a mistake '—not bad. You looked as though you needed the sleep, too.'

He bent, picked up the book and rose to his feet. 'Just resting my eyes,' he said, dismissing her concern as he returned it to the shelves.

There had been a moment when, still drowsy, he'd forgotten the mask, but it was back in place now. She wouldn't be fooled by it though; he could be as grouchy as he liked, she had his number. Quite what she was going to do with it was another matter.

'I'm ready for that cup of tea now,' she said, unwinding, carefully, from the sofa. Or she would be once she'd used the bathroom. 'Can I make one for you?' Then, as she spotted the tea tray set for two, 'Oh.' She reached out and touched the pot. It was stone cold. 'How long have I been asleep?'

He checked his watch. 'A couple of hours. You will let me know if you feel nauseous?'

'You think I went to sleep because I have concus-

sion? Nothing that exciting, I promise you. I was just
tired. I'm afraid I didn't sleep very well last night.'

Cue apology for low-status bedroom, query re mattress, general concern of host over comfort...

Clearly he needed a prompt. 'Please, don't apologise. Really. The bed was fine. I was just worrying
about Maisie.' Then, since that didn't stir him to re-
morse, 'Have you checked to see if the phones are back
on?'

'Not lately,' he admitted. 'Help yourself.'

He indicated a phone on a small writing desk standing by the window.

Unlike its more workmanlike counterpart in the office, this was free of all clutter and contained only a
slender laptop computer and telephone. She lifted the
receiver. There was no dial tone, but the dog, sensing
the possibility of action, came across and then, when
she didn't move, began snuffling beneath the desk, rat-
tling something against the skirting board.

Glancing behind the desk to see what he'd got, she
realised that it was the phone jack. It wasn't plugged
into its socket, but was lying on the floor.

About to tell Harry, she caught sight of Susan and
Maisie, in her ridiculous combination of frilly frock
and rubber boots, hand-feeding carrots to a couple of
donkeys who were leaning over the stone wall that di-
vided the driveway to the house from a field, and, in a
sudden flash of understanding, knew what had happened.

Maisie. She had done this. Gone round the house
quietly disconnecting the phones. Hidden her cellphone. Just to gain a little time.

Was she really that desperate to stay?

'Well?' Harry asked.

She jumped at the nearness of his voice and practically collided with him as she swivelled round to block him from seeing what Maisie had done.

For a moment the room swam and she put out a hand to stop herself from falling.

Harry caught her shoulders to steady her.

'Jacqui?'

As she looked up at him, his face no longer distant, withdrawn, angry, but showing only concern for her, the sensation of falling didn't go away.

'Are you feeling dizzy?'

No... Yes... Not in the way he meant...

'I'm fine,' she said, a little breathlessly. 'Unlike the telephone.'

Cross as she was, all her protective instincts came rushing to the surface. Telling him what Maisie had done would only make things worse between them and she rationalised that a few more minutes wasn't going to change things.

*All she had to do was wait until Harry was safely out of the way, plug it back in and leave him assuming that the telephone people had been working on the line somewhere.*

'Is the line still dead?' he asked.

That small voice that lived in the subconscious urged, 'Tell him...'

She ignored it.

'Er—yes,' she said, fingers mentally crossed as she held up the receiver so that he could listen for himself. 'Not a peep.'

*Although this was technically true, she was well aware from Sunday School that this was something called 'lying by omission' and her voice had that slightly 'peepy' quality that her mother would have recognised instantly. Of course, that might have had more to do with Harry's hand on her shoulder, his closeness, than a total inability to fib without her voice going up several octaves.*

*He took the receiver from her, but maybe he'd learned his lesson from the last time, because he didn't bother to listen, simply replaced it on the cradle.*

'I'd better take another look at your scalp,' he said.

He didn't wait for her permission before he parted her hair with what, for a big bad giant, was exquisite gentleness. But agreeable as this might be, she leaned back—just sufficiently to show him that she could do this without falling over, but not far enough to break contact—and said, 'Can I get this straight? When you say that you're a doctor...'

'Yes?'

'You do mean that you're a doctor of *medicine*?'

Jacqui finally got the smile she'd been waiting for. Genuine humour. The kind of creases around the eyes that looked so good on a man. The kind of creases around the mouth that were so unbelievably sexy...

'That's a very good question, Jacqui. It suggests your brain is still in good working order.'

Oh, good grief, that had to mean the answer was no...

'I'm glad to hear it,' she said. 'Do you have an equally good answer? Or am I to accept from the fact that you evaded giving me one that you are, in fact, a doctor of philosophy? A scholar of some deeply obscure subject such as Babylonian cuneiform, perhaps? Or the breeding habits of natterjack toads? Or even...'

'Relax, Jacqui. Your head is safe in my hands.'

It didn't feel safe. He might know what he was doing, but his careful probing of the damage was sending very unsafe tingles skittering down her spine. But that was what a bang on the head would do for you. Knock things loose. Especially sense; he was the big bad giant who lived at the top of the mountain, she reminded herself...

'Medicine is the family business. My great-grandfather was the local doctor.'

'Really? The village doesn't look big enough to support its own surgery.'

'It used to be in the days when farming was done by men rather than machines. It finally closed about ten years ago when my cousin was lured away to a large practice in Bristol that has its own dedicated team of support staff.'

'Nice for him. Not much fun for the locals. What do they do now?'

'Drive ten miles to the nearest town like most people in rural communities.'

'Definitely no fun if you're old or have a sick child.'

'They should try living in a place where you have to walk for a week...' His jaw clamped down on the words, cutting them off.

So, when he disappeared to foreign parts for months or years, he was working. Africa? Walking for a week to the nearest clinic sounded like rural Africa.

She didn't press him for more details, just stored up the information to take out and examine later.

'So,' she said, verbally tiptoeing around the danger zone, 'that was your great-grandfather. What did your grandfather do?'

'What?' He was back on the defensive, eyes shuttered, expression forbidding, and for a moment she quailed.

'You said it was the family business,' she reminded him.

For a moment she thought he was going to tell her to go to hell and take her busybody nosiness with her.

'He's a heart specialist,' he said, abruptly.

'Present tense?'

'He still takes an active interest in his field,' he said. Then, 'My father is an oncologist and my mother is a specialist in paediatric medicine. Is there anything else you want to know?'

He sounded vaguely surprised to have said so much, she thought. As if he was unused to talking about himself or his family and couldn't quite work out why he was doing it now, and she wondered where all these incredibly clever people were when he so obviously needed them.

'They're all, as you can see, very busy people.'

Like Selina Talbot, then. Obviously putting career before family ran in the family, too.

'And you?' she asked, again leaning back to look up at him.

'I'll just check your vision again.' He took her chin in his hand before she could argue, so that she was forced to keep her head still as he moved his finger across her sight line while she followed it with her eyes. Then, her face still cradled in his hand, he finally answered her. 'I'm a doctor who's satisfied that you've done no serious damage on this occasion but who, if asked for his advice, would suggest taking rather more care when crawling about beneath furniture.' Then, 'And while I'm at it, to avoid walking backwards.'

*That's not what I asked, Harry.*

'I know.'

His palm was cool against her neck and chin, his

thumb, fingers gentle against her cheeks. And everything that was female in her responded with a powerful surge of longing. She wanted him to kiss her, she realised with a shock that left her dizzier than any bang to the head. To touch her. To enfold her in arms that were strong enough to hold off the entire world. *Were* holding off the entire world...

Maybe the blow to her head had done more damage than he thought, because she sensed an equally powerful response from him.

She could almost believe that if one of them didn't speak they might stay like this forever, locked in some fairy-tale enchantment at the top of this misty mountain...

'And?' she persisted, shattering the spell. Fairy tales were for children.

He stirred, then released her. 'I don't have an answer to your question, Jacqui. I no longer know what I am.'

Before she could even begin to formulate a reply, he stepped back, letting his hand drop to his side, putting some space between them.

Now that he'd opened up—if as about as willingly as an oyster surrendering its pearl—she suspected that he felt exposed and vulnerable; that he needed to retreat into the protective shell he'd built around himself. Do some running repairs on the breaches in his defences.

As if to confirm her thoughts, he broke eye contact, looking over her head and out of the window at the safe nothingness offered by the blanket of mist. The distance, mental and physical, only served to demonstrate how close they'd been for that brief moment.

How cold it felt to be separated.

'The mist is clearing. It seems as if you might get some sun after all, before you leave.'

'I'll have my camera ready,' she said, heart sinking as she turned to follow his gaze.

Maisie and Susan were making their way back to the house. The mist was certainly less oppressive and as it swirled patchily she could almost have imagined she caught a glimpse of blue sky.

'I'd better go and rescue Susan,' she said.

And tackle Maisie about the phone. Vickie and Selina Talbot had to be tearing their hair out with frustration.

Not that she was behaving much more responsibly.

She really should have told Harry, but he'd be so angry with the child and a few minutes more or less wouldn't make any difference. As soon as he went off to fiddle with the boiler, or do whatever else he did to fill his day, she'd have the phone plugged back in and Bob, as the saying went, would be her uncle.

She crossed the room, picked up the tray and Harry, as if regretting his earlier confidence and now anxious to be rid of her, crossed quickly to open the door.

'It's nearly lunchtime,' she said. About to suggest he joined them, she thought better of it. She would do her best to bring Maisie and Harry closer together in what time she had, but if she was too obvious about it he'd see right through her. 'Can I get something for you?'

'You should be taking it easy.'

'This *is* easy. I've spent the entire morning asleep in front of the fire while Susan's been doing my job as well as hers.'

No! No… This wasn't a job. She wasn't getting paid. She was doing it because she hadn't got any choice…

'If it'll put your mind at rest,' she added, 'I can

assure you that it won't be anything more exciting than something on toast or a sandwich. Which would you prefer?'

He regarded her through suspiciously narrowed eyes and she knew she'd been wise not to suggest he join them in the kitchen. Then, with something that might have been a shrug, or then again might not, he said, 'If you're making a sandwich, I'll have one in here.'

He left her standing in the doorway, crossed to the desk and flipped open the laptop. Then, as if to demonstrate that he had no intention of moving for the rest of the day, he sat down, thus managing at a single stroke to scupper both her plans.

*Double bedknobs, a broomstick and a dustpan and brush...*

Harry turned on the laptop, determinedly not looking in Jacqui's direction as she left the room.

But the softness of her skin clung to his fingers, the scent of her filled and renewed his body like the air on a soft spring day.

Scarcely appropriate thoughts for a doctor. But then he hadn't thought of himself as that since he'd been shipped home six months earlier at the point of a breakdown. Could scarcely believe his own ears when he heard himself responding to Jacqui's arch question with a 'yes'. As if he'd wanted her to think well of him. He didn't care what she thought of him.

But any more mishaps and he'd take her straight to A&E.

He pulled a face. So much for insisting on her leaving as soon as her car was fixed.

He could hardly insist that she drive back to London today even if the garage did come through with a spare exhaust for her car, the phone connection was restored and Sally could stir herself to make alternative arrangements for Maisie.

He dragged his hand over his face, felt the days-old growth of beard. Was it any wonder that when he'd opened the door to her, Jacqui had looked at him as if he were a monster?

He slammed down the lid of the laptop.

So what if she had.

Anything was better than the pity that had replaced it. He didn't want her pity. He wanted...

The arrival of the garage pick-up rescued him from confronting what exactly he did want, but as he pushed back the chair, glad to escape his thoughts, he saw Jacqui's bracelet lying on the floor beside the desk.

And then, as he bent to pick it up, he saw the telephone jack lying on the floor beside the socket.

# CHAPTER EIGHT

As HARRY approached the kitchen, he heard the sound of laughter. It stopped abruptly as he walked in.

'Susan, a word,' he said, rather more brusquely than he'd intended.

'I'm just off,' she said, taking a headscarf from her pocket. 'I should have been gone half an hour ago.'

'It won't take a minute. I just wanted to ask you to take more care when you're vacuuming.'

She bridled. 'I do my best with the dog hairs. The dogs aren't supposed to go into the library, or the drawing room. The missus won't have it when she's at home. Of course, if I had one of those new cleaners—'

'I'm not talking about dog hairs, woman!'

Harry was confronted by three pairs of female eyes—one pair narrowed with disapproval, one pair dark and very round, one pair framed with slightly raised brows. He ignored the 'could do better' look and concentrated on Susan.

'I know you work extremely hard cleaning up after Sally's strays, but that isn't the problem.'

He had the strangest impression of breath being collectively held behind him.

'Quite the contrary,' he went on. 'In your effort to do a thorough job you appear to have knocked the telephone jack out of the socket in the library. It's why we haven't been able to make or receive calls all morning.'

She frowned. 'But I haven't...'

Out of the corner of his eye he saw a movement but

by the time he'd turned to look at Jacqui she was doing nothing more suspicious than tucking her hair behind her ear.

She gave him that 'What?' look.

A question he didn't want to answer and he turned back to Susan, who, with rare meekness, said, 'I'm sorry, Mr Harry. I'll be more careful in future.'

'No!' Maisie, who'd been sitting at the kitchen table, leapt to her feet, knocking over her chair and sending the hen squawking for safety. 'No!' she repeated. 'You mustn't blame Susan.' She glared at him. 'It was me, OK?' she said, sounding more like a belligerent teen-ager than a six-year-old. 'I did it.'

Maisie?

It was deliberate?

He looked at Jacqui in a bid for some kind of sense and realised that she'd known. Her eyes were liquid, pleading with him to understand, to be kind…

Something that Susan, leaping to Maisie's protection and taking the blame, clearly thought him incapable of.

'What did you do, Maisie?'

'I unplugged the phone.'

'In the library?'

'In the library,' she said, with a touch of defiance. 'In the office. In the kitchen…'

He walked across to the kitchen phone and traced the line to a socket hidden behind a sagging sofa, the plug lying loose on the floor. He didn't ask how she knew what to do—he could well imagine Sally yanking out a plug when she didn't want to take a call—he simply replaced it and stood up.

She might be a little demon, but at least she wasn't prepared to let someone else take the blame for her.

He knew exactly why she'd disconnected the phones,

of course. Jacqui kept telling him why. She didn't want him talking to Selina or Aunt Kate and making other arrangements for her. She wanted to stay here. If he allowed Maisie to tell him that, he'd never be able to send her away…

'Thank you for being so honest,' he said. 'That was very brave of you.' Then, turning to Susan, 'And you are a lot kinder than she deserves. Just leave a note about that cleaner on my desk and I'll see to it.'

There was a sharp rap at the back door, a call of, 'Anyone about?'

'That's the mechanic come to sort out your car,' he said to Jacqui. A welcome distraction. 'Can I trust you to call your agency while I talk to him?' He didn't bother to conceal his anger with her. She was a grown-up and didn't deserve kid gloves. 'They must be very concerned not to have heard from you. Or was the story about the missing cellphone fiction, too?'

He didn't wait for her answer. He wasn't interested in her answer.

She'd known.

She'd looked at him with those big grey eyes, held out the telephone for him to listen to the silence and all the time she'd known what Maisie had done.

As he walked away, he heard the telephone begin to ring. It did not, as anticipated, signal relief. On the contrary, it had a hollow knell-like sound.

'Morning, Dr Talbot.'

The mechanic had loaded Jacqui's car onto the back of his pick-up and was wiping his hands on a rag.

'Mike.' Then, concentrating on the car, 'You're taking her down to the garage?'

'Better get her up on the ramp, have a proper look. Nothing worse than a job half done.'

'No.'

'Do you want me to hang on to it until your visitor leaves? She won't want to be bashing her nice new exhaust to bits going back down the lane, will she?'

He hadn't said anything about a visitor, or that the VW belonged to a woman. But then she'd asked directions at the village shop; the local equivalent of a tabloid headline.

'When will it be ready?'

The sooner it was done, the sooner he could get her disturbing presence out of here. Get back to normal. Or the nearest approximation of it that he could manage.

'Ah, well, I tried to ring earlier. Did you know your phone's out? I did report it.'

'Then your call must have done the trick. It's back on now.'

'Oh, right. Well,' he said, gesturing at the car, 'the problem is that this is an old model. It's going to take a day or two to get hold of the parts, but since I had to come up to tell you, I thought I'd save a trip and take it back with me. Is the delay going to be a problem?'

'Will it make any difference if I say yes?'

'No, but I could organise a rental in the meantime. Something with a higher clearance. If the lady needs a runabout?'

He resisted the temptation. Even if he provided her with alternative transport, where would she go? He had considered suggesting she take Maisie home with her. If she declined, there was no way he could insist. Besides, she might not have room. And if she had, would she admit it?

'We'll manage. Just do it as quickly as you can. And Mike, you'd better ask your brother if he'll fill and roll the potholes in the lane as a temporary measure.' His purpose in neglecting it had been to keep people out, not have them stuck up here unable to leave. 'I'll talk to him about something more permanent as soon as the weather improves.'

'Don't leave it too long. He'll be starting work on the new houses after Easter.'

'New houses?'

'Nice little development. Your Aunt Kate is a canny woman. Pushed through the planning permission on that bottom field by the road. The low-cost housing she insisted on did the trick. It'll keep the youngsters here and save the village school. Mean work for all us.' He nodded in the direction of the house. 'Will you be sending your little girl there?'

His words, so casually spoken, struck like a knife wound straight to the heart.

'No. She's not staying. Give me a call when the car's ready.' And, not waiting for a reply, he turned and walked away. Not back to the house, but up the hill and into the mist.

Jacqui, replacing the receiver, caught sight of her precious car being loaded onto the back of the garage pick-up and, since Harry was nowhere in sight, went outside to find out what was happening.

The mechanic finished securing it and then looked up. 'Morning, miss. This your little beauty?'

She smiled. 'She is lovely, isn't she?'

'A credit to you. Shame you had to bring her up here.'

Unprepared to commit herself, she asked, 'Where are you taking her?'

'Mike's Garage. I'm Mike, by the way.' He extended his hand, then, realising that it was less than clean, thought better of it. 'You'll find us down the lane behind the village shop. I told Dr Talbot that it'll be a couple days before we can get a part. It's her age, you see. Not standard stock. I did offer him a rental in the meantime, but he said not to bother.'

'He did?' Her heart did a little flip-flop that she couldn't quite decipher. Maybe because it meant he wouldn't be bundling her out of the door at the first chance he got. After the way he'd looked at her when he realised she'd known about the phone she'd expected to be thrown out, bag and baggage, at the first opportunity.

'If that doesn't suit you, miss, you just say the word.'

'What? Oh, no.' Then, 'No, really, if I need to come down to the village I'm sure Harry won't mind me borrowing the Land Rover. And I quite understand about the spares. I've had problems in the past. There's no special rush.'

For some reason that appeared to amuse him, but he just said, 'Whatever you say, miss. Do you want to close the gate after me?'

'Of course.'

She waited until he'd driven through then closed it after him before turning back to the house. The mist had thinned sufficiently for her to see how it nestled comfortably in a fold in the hill. No longer threatening, but a sturdy refuge from the worst of the weather.

Beyond it, a movement caught her eye and she saw the dark shape of a man moving swiftly in fierce, angry strides toward the summit.

He had every right to be angry. She should have told him about Maisie's stunt with the phones.

And now she'd compounded her duplicity by encouraging Mike to take his time about fixing the car.

Not that it would make any difference one way or the other since all Vickie had been able to tell her in their brief exchange was that Selina Talbot hadn't responded to her messages, but 'not to worry', she was 'on it'.

Maybe she should make a thorough job of it, call her back and tell her to take her time, too, although she was rapidly coming to the conclusion that it wouldn't make any difference.

Selina Talbot must have known her mother was in New Zealand since it wasn't exactly a last-minute, off-the-cuff trip. She'd been there for five months, for heaven's sake. It would take a desperately casual attitude to communications to miss that one.

Maybe it was paranoia, induced by the bang on her head, but she was beginning to get the strongest feeling that Selina Talbot had known exactly what she was doing. That Harry had been the only responsible adult available and rather than give him the opportunity to say no—and he'd certainly have said no—he'd been presented with a *fait accompli*.

Left holding the baby—nanny included.

Because once she'd come to that conclusion it was equally obvious that, in spite of all her protestations to the contrary, Vickie Campbell—who was not casual about anything to do with her business—must have known exactly what the situation was.

The only thing that completely flummoxed her was the fact that no one had thought to pack some sensible, mucking-about-in-the-country clothes for Maisie.

\*    \*    \*

'The rabbits now. You must come and see the rabbits.'

Jacqui was being given a tour of the menagerie. They'd said hello to the puppies and their mother. Given Fudge an apple and brushed his mane. Taken carrots to the donkeys, who looked as if butter wouldn't melt in their mouths, but, bearing in mind Harry's trouble with them, she'd kept a tight hold of Maisie's hand when she headed for the gate. She had no intention of chasing donkeys all over the hill.

Now she was being dragged into a small paddock behind the stables, where the rabbits and chickens had large and comfortable quarters.

Her reluctance was more to do with the chickens than an unwillingness to visit the rabbits. They were loose, a mix-and-match assortment, busily stalking any worm foolish enough to put its head above ground. She didn't like their sharp little beaks, their beady little eyes or that head-jutting way they walked.

They made her nervous.

The rabbits, more dawn-and-dusk explorers, were taking their time about being tempted to leave the comfort of the hutch and venture into the run.

'Try a carrot, Maisie. Rabbits like carrots, don't they?'

'Not as much as dandelion leaves.'

She jumped as Harry spoke from a few feet behind her. The soft grass had muffled his approach and she'd been so busy keeping an eye on the chickens that she hadn't seen him. She turned round. It was impossible to tell if his hard walk had blown away his temper. His face was giving nothing away.

'Why didn't you tell me, Jacqui?'

Not wanting Maisie to witness what was clearly going to be an awkward conversation, she left her poking a carrot through the wire mesh of the run and walked across to the dry-stone wall at the bottom end of the paddock.

Harry, taking the hint, followed, turning his back to the wall and leaning against it. Waiting for her explanation.

'I knew about the phone no more than five minutes before you. I apologise for not telling you but, having realised it must be Maisie, and aware how much you loathe having her here, I was hoping to save her from your anger.' She looked at him. 'I had intended to deal with it myself at the first opportunity. Would have done it straight away except that you decided to settle in the library.'

'You thought I'd shout at her?'

'It seemed a reasonable assumption.' She glanced at him. 'But actually you don't shout, do you?'

'Despite all appearances, Jacqui, I'm not an ogre.'

She reached out, touched his arm, very lightly as if this would somehow show him that she knew that she'd got it all wrong. Of course he wasn't an ogre. He was unhappy. But then wasn't that the case in most fairy tales?

'I meant, you keep everything bottled up inside. It might be better if you did yell at Maisie. I'm sure she could deal with an emotional outburst a lot better than being frozen out.' She shrugged. 'Whether you can is something else.'

'Amateur psychology I can do without,' he said.

'I'm just telling it the way I see it, but maybe next time you take off into the mist you should try just opening your mouth and letting rip. It's supposed to be therapeutic.'

She held his mocking challenge, refusing to back

down, and in the end he was the one who turned away, looking out into the misty void.

'I can't expect you to understand how desperately difficult I find it...' He made a helpless gesture.

'She's just a little girl, Harry. That she's adopted, a different colour from you, doesn't make her different. She so much wants you to accept her—'

She was going to say 'love her', but thought that might be an emotion too far.

He was already frowning.

'Colour?'

Jacqui swallowed, wishing she hadn't chosen now, this minute, when things were going so well, to bring up the subject. But the words could not be withdrawn. 'She told me.'

'What?' He looked genuinely perplexed. 'What did she tell you?'

And suddenly she had that hideous sinking feeling that came when you realised that you were digging a hole with your mouth. But there was no going back.

'When I tried to explain that I couldn't stay here she asked me if it was because she was adopted. Because of her colour...'

And she looked across at Maisie, crooning to the rabbits, coaxing them out to play. She looked so happy, so relaxed, so different from the little girl who'd delivered that straight-to-the-heart appeal.

'What did she say, Jacqui?'

She held her hand up in front of her, holding him off with a little wave, unable, for a moment, to speak...

'It's OK,' he said. 'I can probably work it out all by myself. She said that I didn't love her, didn't want her because she's adopted, or different. Is that the gist of it?'

She nodded. Then, because she had to know, 'Is it a problem for you?'

He didn't say anything for a while, just stared down at the ground on the far side of the wall. Then, not looking at her, 'Yes, it's a problem.'

What?

She didn't say the word out loud, but maybe her expression was enough.

'When I look at her all I can feel is—'

'No. Not another word.' She took a step back, putting a yard of clear air between them. If he registered the fact it didn't show in his expression. Nothing showed... 'Here I am,' she said, slowly, 'dying of embarrassment for maligning you if only in my thoughts, and you're actually going to stand there and tell me that it's true?'

'I—'

'Look, Jacqui!' Maisie, eyes alight, ran up with something clasped in her hand.

Jacqui gathered herself, then turned round and folded herself up to child height so that she could see what she was holding. Forced herself to smile. To speak normally...

'What have you got there, sweetpea?'

Maisie opened her hands to show a tiny yellow chick. 'Oh,' she said. 'It's pooped on me...'

'That's all we need,' Harry muttered from somewhere far above them. 'Chicks on the loose. Fox heaven—'

'Where did you find it, Maisie?' Jacqui said, interrupting Harry before he said something that would seriously upset the child. Trying to ignore what he'd just told her as she dug a tissue out of her pocket to clean up the mess. Getting a peck for her trouble. Even cute fluffy chicks had beaks...

'Over by the hedge. There are lots of them. Come and see.' She didn't wait, but began to stomp back across the paddock in boots that were at least two sizes too big for her.

'Wait! Be careful, Maisie. You don't want to step on them.'

She might not like chickens much, but she wouldn't want to see one stomped on.

Maisie froze, one leg comically in the air. She was happy, really happy, and Jacqui thought her heart might break for the child...

'We're going to need a cardboard box to put them in. I'm sure I saw one in the mud room.' She turned to Harry, who was still standing by the wall. 'Do you want to get that?'

'You don't want to know what I want,' he said.

'I already do, but don't hold your breath, it's not going to happen any time soon.'

'That sounds as if you know something I don't.'

'First the chickens,' she said. 'Then the bad news.'

# CHAPTER NINE

JACQUI, while grateful for the distraction of rounding up the chicks, nevertheless held her breath as Maisie offered one up to Harry when he returned with the box.

He looked so huge beside her. She looked so vulnerable and she knew he could so easily crush her with an unkind word. But he didn't. After a long moment, he crouched down, placed the box on the ground in front of him and let Maisie tip the chick into his hands.

She looked anxiously up at him for approval.

'Well, what are you waiting for?' he asked. 'Go and find some more.'

Not exactly praise, but Maisie rushed off, tripping over her boots in her eagerness to please him. As Jacqui watched he reached out a hand as if to steady her, but her momentum carried her out of his reach as, the pink ruff of her skirt bouncing, she rushed back to the hedge.

It was over in a second, but the look on his face as he watched her gave the lie to all the hideous feelings of shock and disgust that were whirling around inside her.

As he watched her go, forgetting her prima-donna princess act and just dizzy with excitement like any other six-year-old, his true feelings were etched on his face for the briefest of moments.

Behind the cold, uncaring mask there was exasperation. Amusement, too. But most of all love.

By the time he looked across at her, it had been

wiped out, obliterated, but she wouldn't be fooled again.

'Ouch! Cut it out.' She shook off the annoyed mother hen who had taken exception to their rescue operation and was pecking at her ankles. 'We're taking care of your babies, OK?'

'I *told* you to wear wellies,' Maisie told her in passing—and sounding exactly like a grown-up telling some little kid 'I told you so'.

Harry caught her eye. 'That had better not be a smile,' she warned him.

'Not even close,' he assured her.

Hmm.

Ten minutes later, as she placed the last chick in the box, she said, 'That seems to be the lot. Where do we put them?'

'In the stables. Here, take the box.' He pushed it into her arms and she thought he was done, but he said, 'I'll go and look for some boards to keep them penned in.'

'They'll need food and water,' Maisie reminded him, still buzzy with excitement and forgetting to be cool and distant.

'You're right. Do you want to see to that?'

Her shoulders went up to her ears in an absolute paroxysm of joy at being given something important to do by Harry, and she rushed off.

'What are you looking so pleased with yourself for?' he demanded, looking up and catching her in a grin that, unlike him, she was not quick enough to hide.

'Me?' Jacqui asked.

'The words "Cheshire" and "cat" come to mind.'

Not quite the image she was striving for, but she kept the smile glued to her face and said, 'I have a naturally sunny disposition, Harry.' Then added, 'You'd better get used to it.'

'Is that your way of telling me that you're going to be around for some time?'

'That's the bad news, yes. Your cousin hasn't responded to the messages left by the agency, so unless you have some better plan, you're stuck with us.'

He didn't leap to assure her that her self-sacrifice was appreciated. He didn't say anything.

'Of course,' she went on, 'she may have decided to get in touch with you direct. It's entirely possible that while you've been wherever it is you've been and we've been out here having a good time with these adorable chickens, she's left a message on your answering machine.' She was finding it increasingly difficult to keep up the businesslike manner in the face of his totally blank expression. 'It's even possible that she didn't wait to call us, but boarded a plane home the minute she picked up the first message.'

'I hope you're not holding your breath on that one,' he said, finally.

'No. Taking my cues from those who know and love her, I've kept breathing in and out on a regular basis.'

'Smart woman,' he said. Then, 'Will you stay?'

He was asking her? Actually asking her to stay?

'Can you stay?' he went on, when she didn't immediately answer. 'I realise that we're all taking you completely for granted.'

'No...'

'No?'

'Yes...' She gathered herself. 'You're not taking me for granted. That honour belongs to someone else. And yes, of course I'll stay for as long as I'm needed.' And she discovered she was smiling again.

'Thank you,' he said. 'I'll book a replacement holiday for you myself as soon as things are back to normal.'

She shrugged. 'Maisie said this is a good place for a holiday and, despite the weather and the chickens, I can see why she likes it. Besides, the sun is so bad for your skin.'

'It isn't always like this,' he said, turning away and heading for the paddock gate, opening it and standing back so that she could go ahead of him. She turned in the opening, blocking his way. What she had to say could wait, but he would keep taking to the hills.

'While you're here, can I just get a few things straight?'

'Will anything I say stop you?'

She ignored the rudeness—now she recognised it as a defence mechanism it was easy to ignore—and smiled, as if he'd said something amusing.

'Since I'll be here for a while, I'm going to have to ask you to let me know when you're going to disappear the way you did at lunchtime.'

'I was under the impression that you were Maisie's nanny, not mine.'

'Were you?' She wasn't anyone's nanny, but she didn't see any need to tell him that. Then, 'It's just a question of next of kin, in the event of an accident, illness, that's all. I'll also need a list of essential telephone numbers, a designated vehicle to use in an emergency—my own motor insurance will cover me—and a set of keys for both the house and the car.'

'Anything else?'

'Yes,' she said. 'You missed lunch. You'll find some sandwiches in the fridge when you're done.'

With that she turned and walked away.

'Jacqui…' She halted, waiting for the explosion. When none came, she glanced back. 'How's your head?'

She looked back over her shoulder. He hadn't moved and for a moment she was tempted to do a 'Maisie', wince a little, get him closer to have another look. But she just said, 'You did a good job, doc.' Her voice was a little husky and she was forced to clear her throat before she added, 'I'll recommend you to all my friends.'

And then, very much afraid she was doing the Cheshire Cat thing again, she raised the box containing the chicks a little, to indicate that she'd better get on.

Her powerhouse smile rocked Harry back on his feet. It was only his hand, grasping the bracelet in his pocket, that kept him grounded. He'd meant to give it straight back to her when he found it, but the business with the telephones had knocked it clean out of his head and then he'd taken off for the hilltop as if the higher he climbed the further away he was from everything that reminded him of everything he'd lost.

Except that today he'd found himself drawn back. Not just to Maisie, but to Jacqui.

Then, stuffing his hands into his pockets to keep himself from just reaching out for her, he'd found the bracelet. That was why he'd called out. To give it to her.

His fingers tangled with the chain, his thumb rubbed over the tiny heart.

He took it out and looked at it again. '…forget and smile…'

Who was she supposed to forget?

He wanted to ask her whether she'd managed it. And

if so what the trick of it was. But maybe she was finding it as difficult as he was and he put the chain back in his pocket.

Much safer not to go there.

He'd leave it somewhere for her to find.

Later, when the chicks were safe and he'd somehow managed to avoid sitting down to eat supper with Maisie, instead making do with the sandwiches Jacqui had left for him earlier while he caught up with the estate accounts in the office, he picked up the telephone in another attempt to contact his cousin. Despite her willingness to stay, he couldn't take advantage of Jacqui's good nature.

And yet as he put the receiver to his ear, he found himself almost wishing the phone were dead again.

No such luck.

He got her first time.

'Harry?' Sally sounded almost as unhappy to hear from him as he was to be calling her. 'Have you any idea what time it is here?'

He thought about it. 'Two, three o'clock in the morning?' he offered. 'Were you asleep?'

'Of course I was asleep!'

Of course she was. He hadn't called in the middle of the night simply to be annoying. He knew if she'd been thinking clearly she would have ignored his call.

'I've called about Maisie.'

'Oh,' she said.

'The agency and the nanny accompanying her thought she was going to be staying with Aunt Kate, Sally.'

'Really? Why? I merely asked for them to deliver her to her grandmother's house. They've done it before.'

'You're not getting the picture here, Sally. These are responsible people who take their duties seriously. They won't leave her with just anyone.'

'You're not just anyone, though, are you?'

'She's your responsibility, Sally,' he said, refusing to go there. 'A little girl. You can't treat her like one of your strays. You'll have to fax a note to the agency, giving them written permission to leave her here with me.'

'All right! OK. Consider it done.' Then, 'Is that it, only there won't be enough concealer in the entire world to cover the dark shadows under my eyes if I don't get some sleep? I mean, she's not sick or anything?'

'And if she is? Will you drop everything and come home?'

'Don't be silly, darling, she wouldn't want me. She never wants me. Besides, you know how hopeless I am at that sort of thing.'

There were any number of things he knew and he was tempted to say all of them, but what would be the point?

'When will you be home?'

'Not for a month at least. I'm going on to Japan from here and then to the States to shoot some commercials. After that I'm going to spend a little time on a friend's yacht. I sooo need a holiday.'

'What about Maisie? Don't you think she might like to join you?'

'Maisie? What on earth would she do on a yacht?'

He didn't ask what she'd be doing. Her romance with a billionaire playboy was currently top of the hot-gossip pops and she clearly didn't want a precocious child getting in the way.

'A month,' he said. 'Right.'

'Well, maybe just a little bit longer. It depends on whether the decorators have finished the house.'

'Decorators?'

'It's going to be featured in a magazine later in the year so interior designers are falling over themselves to do it for me for the publicity. It's supposed to be finished by Easter, but you know how these things can run over.'

'I have heard,' he agreed, finally understanding why Maisie couldn't just stay at home with Sally's retinue of staff to take care of her, the way she usually did. 'Would you like to talk to Maisie?'

'I'm really tired, Harry.'

'Jacqui, then?'

'Who?'

'The nanny who brought her here.'

'What? But I thought… Wasn't she supposed to be going on holiday?'

'Yes. She missed her plane because of your incompetence and now she's given up her holiday to stay and look after Maisie.'

'For heaven's sake, Harry, why did you let her do that? You're perfectly capable of looking after one small child, aren't you?'

'I didn't let her do anything. She insisted. I guess she just goes that extra mile for a child in her care,' he said, answering the first question. He ignored the second, since they both knew the answer to that one.

'Vickie Campbell did say that she's a gem. She's hoping to persuade her to take on the job full-time.'

'Is she? Well, I hope for Maisie's sake that she succeeds.'

Because the fact that Jacqui Moore was taking care of her was the only thing he was happy about.

He briefly considered calling his aunt, but while waking Sally in the middle of the night had been a deliberate strategy to catch her off guard, disturbing Kate at the crack of dawn in New Zealand to listen to his concerns was something else.

And what could she do, anyway? Abandon the first proper holiday she'd had in years just because he wanted to keep his distance? She'd get on the next flight if he asked her, he knew that, but it was bad enough that her daughter treated her like an unpaid servant.

That was the problem with occupying the high moral ground. You couldn't walk away when things got difficult.

Jacqui was staying. Maisie was happy. As for him…well, right now all he needed was a hot bath to ease the nagging aches that were always brought on by the damp weather. If he was very lucky Jacqui might even have left him some leftovers from supper to re-heat—since she seemed to have taken it upon herself to make sure he was eating properly.

He was still smiling at the thought when, at the top of the stairs, he paused, transfixed by the intermingled sounds of splashing and shrieks of laughter floating down to him from the floor above.

It sounded so joyful, so *normal*, and he took a step closer.

'One, two, three…' The water whooshed through Maisie's hand and she shrieked with laughter as it splashed over the edge of the bath in a tidal wave.

Jacqui grabbed a towel to stop the flood, but as she

dropped it on the floor she confronted a pair of large feet encased in nothing but a pair of what were now extremely wet socks.

'Oh,' she said, looking up. 'Sorry. We were having a waterspout competition.' Then, because as he'd already pointed out she never did know when to stop, 'Want to play?'

'You're planning to flood us out?'

'It's not coming through the ceiling, is it?' she asked, scrambling to her feet.

'No, really, it's OK. I didn't mean to stop you having fun. I just came to return this.' He took the bracelet from his pocket. 'I found it in the library. I thought you might be worrying about it.'

Jacqui looked at her wrist, not quite able to believe that it had been gone all that time and she hadn't even missed it.

'I noticed you wearing it,' he said. 'Earlier.'

'Did you? Yes. Thank you.'

'Interesting inscription.'

'You read it?' Then, 'It practically needs a magnifying glass.'

'I've got twenty-twenty vision.'

From behind her Maisie, in a loud stage whisper, said, 'Ask him now.'

'Ask me what?'

Jacqui, about to tell him, was stopped by a warning finger.

'Maisie?' Harry prompted.

Maisie, suddenly not so sure of herself, began playing with a plastic duck, pushing it beneath the water and letting it bob up. 'About what Susan said this morning.'

He knelt down beside the bath, ignoring the water

soaking into his trousers, and captured the duck, held on to it so that she was forced to look at him. 'Susan said a lot of things this morning.'

She mumbled something. He waited. 'About going to school in the village,' she repeated, crossly.

'You'd really like to go?' Her face said it all. 'But what would you wear? You can't go to school in a party frock.'

'Why not?'

'Because,' Jacqui said, hurriedly intervening, 'it would make all the other little girls unhappy because they didn't have something that pretty.'

'Oh. Right.' Then, 'There are those old clothes you found,' she said, looking up, eyes wide, a little tremble to the voice, then switching her appeal back to Harry and saying, 'Pleeease.'

She never used his name, Jacqui realised. Most children in her position would have called him 'Uncle Harry', surely?

Harry didn't immediately answer, but turned to her and said, 'What do you think, Jacqui?'

She did her best to ignore the little butterfly that was waltzing around in the region of her abdomen at this evidence of trust. The truth was more likely to be more prosaic. By putting the decision in her hands, he could dissociate himself from the fallout if the whole experiment was a disaster.

She was afraid that it might well be. A child of six who had never been to school would find the situation challenging to say the least. Especially if she was a little princess like Maisie.

But if she did go to school, she'd be out of Harry's hair for most of the day. And if it went well, he would find it very difficult to change his mind about her staying.

Which meant she'd just have to do everything she could to ensure it went well.

'If the head teacher doesn't mind taking her for the last couple of weeks of term, I'm sure she'd enjoy the company,' she said. Then, because arriving at school wearing ill-fitting cast-offs would be just as bad as turning up in a yellow silk frock and satin Mary Janes, she added, 'There is just one problem. I did notice on my way through the village that the children all seemed to be wearing a fairly basic kind of uniform. Grey skirts, white shirts, red sweaters.' Then, because she knew that it all had to be spelled out so there could be no misunderstanding, 'Sensible shoes.'

'Black?'

'Or brown.'

'Sensible black or brown shoes?' He shook his head as if unable to believe it. 'And dreary grey skirts, too. Well, I guess that changes everything. Maisie wouldn't want to wear anything like that.'

He stood up, clearly thinking that was an end to it, and, for a heartbeat, Jacqui seriously considered committing grievous bodily harm.

Maisie forestalled her, leaping to her feet, flinging her arms wide and sloshing water in all directions as she declared, 'Yes, I would!' As if not quite believing it herself, she blinked, then said, 'I *want* a uniform. I like grey.'

Harry, halfway to the door, stopped, turned back. 'You're really sure? There's no point in Jacqui taking you into town to buy you school clothes if you're going to change your mind.'

'Please, please, please!' she begged.

Jacqui turned to him, planning to add her own appeal, but just in time saw the tiny tucks at the corners of his mouth that betrayed him.

He'd actually made Maisie plead for clothes that she'd normally die rather than wear, she realized, and she wasn't sure whether she was mad at him, or overwhelmed with admiration for such a slick piece of psychological string-pulling.

Maybe he thought she was going to say something, because he put out a warning hand to stop her.

'OK, if that's what you want, I'll ring the head teacher and ask her if she'll take you. But be very sure it's what you want. Once you start, you can't change your mind.'

'I won't, I won't!'

Harry glanced at her then and Jacqui realised that the I-don't-want-to-know disguise had slipped again. His smile—a combination of tenderness, solicitude and a pleased-with-himself look that was totally endearing—lit up his face and, without even thinking about it, she put her hand on his arm, stretched up on her toes and kissed his cheek.

For a moment there was an illusion of time stopping. There was no sound, no movement, not even from Maisie. It was as if a single heartbeat of time was being stretched to infinity as his smile faded into something immeasurably deeper.

It was a moment of pure magic; as if she could suddenly see right through the protective shell with which he armoured himself against the world, and for a moment she felt pure joy. And then she shivered as, at the heart of him, she confronted the hollow, black centre of true pain.

It was so negative a force that she lost her balance,

as if blown back by the shock of it, but even as she wobbled off her toes he caught her, held her steady, one strong arm around her waist.

The smile had completely disappeared now and his voice was soft, barely audible as he said, 'You take terrible risks, Jacqui Moore.'

She swallowed, well aware of the risks she was running with her fragile heart, and said, 'Nothing worth having,' she said, 'is without risk.'

'I know,' he said. 'But once you've taken the risk, you have to live with the consequences.'

# CHAPTER TEN

HARRY knew he was playing with fire. Despite his surly manner, his strenuous efforts to keep his distance, she hadn't been discouraged, but had continued to reach out to him, had finally touched him. Not just physically, but in the dark and shuttered place where no one had been in the last five years.

Not even him.

Each time he saw her, spoke to her, spent time with her, she got a little closer, sneaking beneath his guard, involving him—and not just with Maisie. She might not have an umbrella like Mary Poppins, but there was something magical about her.

Why wasn't she afraid of him?

Everyone else seemed to get the 'keep out' message, but she persistently ignored it. And now she'd kissed him and he had his arm around her—again—and the only thing on his mind was kissing her back.

Really kissing her.

He should have let her fall back into the bath. Better still, flung himself into it. The water wasn't cold, but it would have served to douse the heat that flooded his veins whenever he was within touching distance of her.

She was wrecking all the effort he'd put into getting his life back on an even keel. The hard work he'd put into blocking out all emotion so that he could get back out in the field. Do his job.

She was seriously bad for his peace of mind and he should put a stop to this right now, but heaven help him she was lovely and the goodness and warmth that emanated from her called to him like the hearth on a cold winter night.

As he continued to hold her, torn between head and heart, her lids fluttered down and with eyes closed, soft lips slightly parted, she gave a little sigh. And he knew that no power on earth could save him.

Jacqui felt the fleeting brush of Harry's lips against her own. Scarcely a kiss in any true sense, just enough to prove his point and demonstrate the danger she was in. Too late. Brief though it was, it had the power to stir her body, lifting it from languor as the first rays of spring sunshine opened the primrose, and her heart leapt with a recklessness that was terminal.

And, looking up into the burnished heat of his eyes, she understood that, while Harry Talbot had been guarding his heart against all-comers, she had given hers away.

'Excuse me! If you're going to be doing gross stuff like kissing—'

'No!' Jacqui recovered first, turning abruptly, and, grabbing a towel from the rail, swept it around Maisie and lifted her out of the water and began to rub her dry. 'I lost my balance, that's all, and Uncle Harry caught me.'

Maisie gave her a do-you-think-I'm-a-total-idiot look, then turned to Harry and, without any expression at all said, 'He's not my uncle. He's my daddy.'

Her mind had clearly been doing its subconscious thing with the 'uncle' title and it had just slipped out while her mind was still away somewhere in dream-land…dreaming.

And had totally backfired.

Harry froze. What on earth had Sally been telling

the child? What fanciful fairy stories had she been weaving in her head?

And guilt speared through him, as real a pain as anything he'd suffered, taking his breath as it drove into his heart. He'd surrendered this child of his heart to a woman who treated her as little more than an accessory. He'd walked away without a fight, giving up all right to her love, her respect. What could he say now that wouldn't make things worse than they already were?

Something. He had to say something and quickly because Jacqui's silver-grey eyes were asking the obvious question and demanding nothing less than the truth.

'Jacqui…' he began. Faltered.

Her expression changed from confused query to hard certainty and she said, 'Excuse me, Harry. It's late and I need to get Maisie into bed if we're going shopping tomorrow.' And she picked the child up in her arms and swept past him.

A few minutes ago he'd been mentally bemoaning the fact that this woman had breached the defensive wall he'd built against all emotional ties and was busy dismantling it brick by brick.

Now she had withdrawn and it was like the sun going in.

He tried to say something, but it was too late. She'd gone. And so had Maisie.

For a moment he was tempted to go after them, demand a fair hearing. But what was fair? He'd done what he'd done and there was no way to change that.

Maybe it was better this way. He should just go and have the shower he'd been planning and stay out of everyone's way for their sakes, as well as his. Return to what passed for normality in his life.

But he was drawn to the murmur of voices from the tower bedroom, as he'd been drawn earlier to their laughter. The soft reassurance of Jacqui's voice as she put the child to bed. Maisie's desperate, 'I'm sorry, I'm sorry… I didn't mean to say it. He won't make me leave, will he? I can still go to school—'

He tapped, pushed open the door. Felt his heart turn over at the sight of Maisie tucked up in her 'princess' bed, his throat seize and tighten. But they were looking at him, waiting for him to speak.

'Come and see me before you go shopping tomorrow, Jacqui,' he said, forcing the words past the lump in his throat. 'You'll need money.'

He sensed Jacqui looking at him, knew she was searching for some clue as to what he was thinking. He hoped, when she'd worked it out, she'd let him know, because he'd abandoned the script he'd written for himself and was floundering about in the dark, looking for some spark of light to show him the way.

'I'd feel happier if you came, too,' she said. 'I'm hopeless at finding my way around strange cities.'

And there it was. His light in the darkness…

'Of course,' he said, and, doing his best to ignore the straight-to-the-heart appeal, added, 'Do you know what she'll need?'

'I'll make a list.' He nodded, turned to leave. 'Harry…' He waited. 'I left some supper for you. In the fridge.' And the light flared into something brighter, something warmer.

Harry felt as if he'd been waiting hours before Jacqui found him, manoeuvring a tray around the library door.

'I've made coffee.'

'You didn't have to do that,' he said, taking it from her, putting it on the sofa table. Or maybe she did. The tray, coffee, were nothing but props, he realised, something to occupy her so that she could avoid looking directly at him. It was only now, when she wasn't doing it, that he understood just how direct her gaze was.

Little wonder she could see right through him. Dismiss the mask for what it was.

Having just seen himself clearly for the first time in what seemed like years, he didn't blame her for not wanting to look at him now.

She poured coffee into two cups, handing him his black and unsugared without asking, then took the armchair on the far side of the fireplace and waited for him to join her. Sit down and face the music.

Well, OK, he hadn't expected to get away without some explanation. If she hadn't found him, he wouldn't have sought her out, but he would deny with his last breath that he was hiding from her; if that had been the case he'd have done a much better job of it. But he'd done with hiding from himself or anyone else.

But then again, maybe he was lying to himself about that, too.

'You must be wondering—'

'Yes, I am, but before you start, Harry, I think I should tell you that Maisie and I have had a bit of a chat about disconnecting telephones, telling the truth, that sort of thing. She owned up to hiding my cellphone and to emptying her bag and replacing the sensible clothes her mother had packed for her with her prettiest clothes. It seemed she wanted you to notice her.'

'You can tell her that she succeeded.'

'I suggest you tell her that yourself.'

Jacqui, he could see, was not amused, but then he hadn't expected her to be. He was in deep trouble and not just on account of Maisie.

'First thing,' he promised.

'So far, so good. It's downhill from there. In fact she was extremely cross that I thought she might be getting a little carried away by the whole fairy-tale thing—' she reached into her pocket and took out a folded sheet of paper '—which is why she gave me her birth certificate.'

'Her birth certificate?' Shocked, he said, 'What on earth is she doing with that? It should be locked up.'

Out of harm's way.

'She said she found it "lying around". I suspect the truth is that she searched for it, maybe took advantage of an open office safe.' She smiled and he forgot to breathe. 'I don't know about you, but I'm confident of Maisie's ability to arrange a suitable distraction if she wanted something badly enough.'

'She is a bit of a handful,' he agreed. And discovered that, despite everything, he was smiling back.

'And in case you were wondering why, I'd say she was trying to find out who she is.'

His smile was short-lived. 'She knows who she is.'

'You think so? If you were her, wouldn't you have a few questions?'

'She should have asked Sally.' Then, realising how pointless an exercise that would have been—if anyone lived in a fantasy world it was his cousin—he said, 'Her birth certificate won't tell her anything.'

'No?' Jacqui opened the long, narrow document across her lap. 'I'd say this little piece of paper tells us quite a lot. For instance, it's not your average run-of-the-mill birth certificate. It's not even an adoption certificate, but a consular birth certificate issued in Digali, a small sub-Saharan country that's been in the throes of a civil war for years.' She looked up, the firelight dancing in her eyes as she challenged him across the hearth. 'You were working there?'

'For an international medical charity, yes.'

'Really?' Her interest was immediate. Then, with a barely perceptible sigh, 'How I envy you.'

'You should have stayed on at university and qualified if you'd wanted to nurse in the field. Heaven knows, there's need enough.'

'I know, but life has a habit of getting in the way.' She seemed to drift away for a moment and, although she was smiling, he thought it was the saddest thing he'd ever seen. Full of regret. Loss. And the walls around his heart that she'd been so determined to dismantle crumbled of their own accord.

'Will you tell me?' he asked. Because he wanted to know, needed to know what had happened to make her look so sad, before he could begin to think how to make it better.

She came back, looked at him for a moment and then said, 'Maybe. Later.'

Depending on how frank he was with her? He had no intention of lying to her.

'Is that a promise?' he asked, leaning forward in his chair, holding his breath as he waited for her answer, and when, at last, she replied with a single nod he knew that it wasn't an easy decision, that she'd thought hard before she'd decided to trust him.

Her expression, too, was deeply serious. And then something sparkled in her eyes as she said, 'It's a deal, Harry. You tell me your secrets and I'll tell you mine.'

'My secrets are there, on your lap, in a public doc-

ument that anyone with the price of a copy from the
Public Record Office can see.'

'I'll want to know more than the plain fact that
you're a liar, Harry Talbot.'

The words were harsh, her voice was not. Nor were
her eyes. He didn't answer and she said, 'OK. Let's
see.' She glanced at Maisie's birth certificate and began
to read.

'Father: Henry Charles Talbot. Occupation: Surgeon.
Mother: Rose Ngei. Occupation: none. Baby's name:
Margaret Rose. Place of birth—'

She made a small dismissive gesture with one hand
and said, 'How did you do it, Harry?' Then, 'Why did
you do it?'

'Because I wasn't prepared to let Maisie become just
another statistic of war.'

'There must have been dozens of babies.
Hundreds—'

'Thousands,' he said. 'It's always the innocent that
suffer most.'

'So why her?'

He shook his head, for a moment unwilling to relive
the horror. He wanted to get up, walk out of the room,
lose himself in the hills, but that was what he'd been
doing for years. Running away, burying himself in
work. The fact that he'd finally run himself to a stand-
still, burned out, proved that it wasn't the answer. And
changing locations hadn't made one jot of difference.

But he'd kept it buried for too long to be able to
easily find the words. Instead he knelt before the fire,
stirred the ashes with a poker, tossed on a couple of
logs, watching while they smouldered, caught, burst

into flame. Delaying the moment for as long as possible.

She didn't press him. Remained perfectly silent while he organised his thoughts, and eventually there was nothing left to do but begin.

'Her mother was a refugee fleeing from the fighting,' he said. 'I never knew her name—I made that up.' He glanced at her to make sure she understood and she reached out, touched his shoulder to show that she did. 'I don't even know where she came from, only that she had the misfortune to blunder into a minefield. She was brought into a field hospital we'd set up. She and her baby were all but dead when I got to her. All I could do was deliver Maisie with an emergency section.'

Jacqui said nothing, just covered her mouth with her hand to smother words that she knew were meaningless; understanding the horror of the picture he'd sketched without any need for him to fill in the hideous details.

'Maisie was small, weak, but as I lifted her scrawny little body from what was left of her mother and wiped her clean, she gave a cry of such...*triumph*. It was as if she was saying, "I've made it! I'm alive!" And she gripped my finger as if she'd never let it go. In that awful place it seemed like a miracle, Jacqui.'

'It was. You'd saved her.'

'But for what? The reality of the situation was that she wouldn't last one day in a refugee camp without a mother to care for her.'

'But she did survive.'

'I made her a promise that she wouldn't become just another nameless casualty of a pointless war.'

'You saved her,' she whispered again. 'How did you do that?'

'I kept her with me. She slept beside me, travelled next to me. I fed her, cared for her and on occasion I operated with her slung in a carrier on my back.'

He must have shuddered as he thought about how close he'd come to losing her because without seeming to move Jacqui was suddenly on her knees beside him, taking his hand between hers, holding it for a moment, before putting her arm around his neck and drawing him close, cradling him against her breast.

'Tell me,' she whispered fiercely against his neck. 'Tell me what happened to you.'

Her warmth, her scent, seemed to seep into his bones, restoring something inside him that he'd done his best to kill. It hurt, but in the way a wound did when it was healing.

'Every moment of it is so clear,' he said.

The heat of the late afternoon. The dust. The flies. The warm weight of Maisie slung across his back...

'The clinic had just finished and I was walking back to my quarters in the compound,' he began. 'Maisie woke, began to grizzle and I stopped, took her out of the sling, had her in my arms. The last thing I remember is her little face lighting up in this great big smile...' He shook his head. 'Then the world blew apart as a shell landed somewhere behind us and I was thrown forward by the blast.'

'Maisie? She was unhurt?'

'When the bombardment stopped they found me in the shelter, hunched over her, protecting her. I must have crawled there, although I don't remember how I got there—'

'You saved her again.'

'A moment earlier...'

'Sssh,' she said, on her knees beside him. 'You

saved her.' Then, as she stroked his back as if to comfort him, she said, 'Oh!' as she made the connection. 'That's what happened to your back...'

Finally she faltered and he was the one offering her comfort, holding her close. 'Forget it,' he said. 'Forget you ever saw it.'

'No!' She pulled back. 'I want to see. Now.' And without waiting, she began to unbutton his shirt. He grabbed at her hands to stop her but she kept hold of his shirt, looked up at him, held her ground until he lifted his hands free, let her do what she wanted. She leaned forward then, kissed him so sweetly that the urgent response from a body already overloaded with stimuli seemed...profane.

Then, as he caught his breath, doing his best to cope with a need that left him utterly defenceless, she carried on unbuttoning his shirt, tugging it out of his waistband, pushing it back until it fell on the floor.

And then she touched him.

Tentatively at first, her fingertips outlining his shoulders, his arms, then bolder as she flattened her hands, sliding her palms over the mess of scar tissue.

Finally she leaned into him, her arms around him, fingertips tracing each place where the blast had ripped the flesh from his back.

'Does it hurt?' she asked.

Hurt? With her cheek pressed against his chest, her hair brushing his cheek, he was beyond feeling anything but the hard, heavy ache of his turgid penis pressing against his zipper.

'Yes,' he managed—not a lie; he was in pain, but it wasn't his back that was hurting—and pulled his shirt back on.

She sat back on her heels, a tiny frown puckering

the space between those lovely eyes, and he abandoned his shirt buttons to reach out, smooth it away.

'Don't,' he said. 'Don't frown. I'm fine.'

She looked up at him, eyes huge and dark in the firelight. 'Are you? So why is Maisie living with your cousin? And why are you so unhappy?'

'Unhappy?' He leaned back against the chair to put some distance between them. Took a sip of the luke-warm coffee, giving himself time to gather himself, time to think.

'You're not going to deny it?'

'No, I'm not going to deny it, but it's as you said. Life gets in the way. My injuries were too extensive to be treated locally but I refused to be shipped home without Maisie and that was a problem because she didn't have any papers. I had no rights. I needed another miracle.'

'And you got one.'

'When it became a matter of life or death, the head of the medical unit sent for the consul to try and talk some sense into me. A truly compassionate man, he stopped me from explaining the situation, just produced his register of births and suggested it was time my little girl was registered. He didn't ask me the father's name, he merely asked me for mine and filled it in. By the time he'd got to the mother's name, I'd caught up. I even gave Maisie my mother's name, which he seemed to appreciate. And when that was done, he gave me a copy of the certificate and congratulated me on my new daughter.' He met her gaze head-on. 'She is mine, Jacqui. In every way that matters, and I'd have done a lot worse than lie to a consular official to keep her with me.' And because, somehow, it was important to convince her, he said the words that he had never before uttered out loud. 'I loved her, Jacqui. Love her. There was no way I could just hand her over to an orphanage, no matter how well-run.'

'Of course you couldn't. You brought her home, here to Hill Tops.'

'I wish. The truth is that after I was medevac'd home, I spent a ridiculously long time in hospital. Skin grafts, that sort of thing. Sally stepped into the breach, took Maisie in, hired a nanny, had fun dressing her up in lovely clothes.'

'Like playing dolls,' Jacqui said. 'But with a real little girl.'

'Inevitably some newshound got wind of it, managed to take some photographs of her with this small black child, and within days the rumours were all over the papers like a rash. Not that anyone thought to tell me.'

'So she pretended she'd adopted this little war orphan.'

'The truth would have exposed the lie. She did it to protect me. To protect Maisie.' He owed his cousin that. Then, 'Besides, all the big stars were doing it at the time. It was good PR.'

'You must hate her so much.'

He shook his head. 'No, I just know her, that's all. It's why she avoids me at all costs.'

'And Maisie?'

'By the time I was fit enough to reclaim her, she had a new life. I didn't like it much, but I couldn't take her back overseas with me, into war zones, famine-stricken areas where her own life would be at risk.'

'You could have stayed at home with her.'

'Maybe I would have, if things had been different. But I'd been out of her life for so long that she'd forgotten me. Treated me like a stranger.'

'She hadn't forgotten you, Harry. She thought you'd abandoned her and she was punishing you for that.'

He managed a smile. 'Neat and tidy psychology, Jacqui, but just a little heavy on wishful thinking, don't you think?'

'Possibly. But you have to ask yourself one question. If she's forgotten you, why did she tell me that she's going to be a doctor when she grows up?'

His heart lifted a beat. 'When? When did she tell you that?'

'On the way here. I asked her if she was going to be a model, like her mother, and she put me right in double-quick time. She was going to be a doctor, like…'

'Like?'

'She stopped, didn't finish the sentence. Have you noticed how she does that? Half tells you things. I realise now that she once came very close to telling me that she knew her grandmother wasn't here. The thing about Maisie is that you have to know the right questions to ask.'

'She gets that from Sally, who certainly knew her mother wasn't here.'

'You've spoken to her?'

'Earlier. She said something odd, too. She said you weren't supposed to stay. Seemed quite irritated by your dedication to duty.'

'Really?' She smiled. 'I wonder why that was? Let me see… Could it be that she wanted you to have a chance to get close to Maisie again? Re-establish the closeness you once had?'

'Are you suggesting that she's got tired of playing mother and wants to offload her so that she can play house, undisturbed, with the billionaire?'

'You know her, I don't. Is she really that shallow?' When he didn't answer, she said, 'One thing I do know, Harry. Maisie really wants to stay here with you. Maybe Sally knows that, too.' She reached out, laid her hand over his. 'Maybe, despite all evidence to the contrary, in your cousin's case beauty really is more than skin deep.'

He looked at her, shook his head, as if he was lost for words.

'What?'

'I was just wondering how you got to be so wise.'

'I wish.' And she wrapped her hand around the chain on her wrist, holding it against her heart.

'Tell me,' he said. 'Tell me about him.'

'Him?'

'Not a him?'

She shook her head and that was the moment he understood how utterly defenceless he was.

He might, in time, be able to overcome the memory of a man, but how could he compete with a woman…?

'I promised, didn't I?' she said, as if regretting it.

'You did and I'll bet you've never broken a promise in your life.'

'Once. Just once. I promised Emma I'd never leave her but in the end I didn't have a choice.' She unfastened the bracelet, held it up. 'I had this made for her birthday last month. I wanted her to know that it was all right to forget me, move on.' She let it curl into her palm. Closed her hand over it. 'Her family sent it back.'

'Her family?'

She looked up at him, her expression puzzled, and he suddenly realised what she was saying. Emma was not a lover, but a child.

'How long were you her nanny?' he said, quickly, before she caught up, worked out what he'd been thinking.

'Years. Too long, perhaps.' Then, gathering herself, she said, 'You asked why I dropped out of university. I did it for Emma.' She looked up at him. 'I think you're probably the only person I know who'd understand why.'

'I'll take that as a compliment.'

'Believe me, it was meant that way.' She turned away, as if it was too painful to continue, reaching for her untouched coffee, putting off the moment.

He caught her hand, stopping her. 'Leave it, it's cold,' he said, and, standing up, he pulled her to her feet. 'I'll make some more.' Then, 'Or are you going to give me another lecture about drinking coffee late at night?'

She managed a smile. 'I'm having enough trouble telling you the story of my life.'

'Then I'll add a little something to it to ease the pain,' he said, picking up a bottle from the tray on the sideboard on the way out and handing it to her, so that he could open the door. There was no way he was letting go of her hand until she was safely in the kitchen.

He shooed the hound off the sofa, lowered her into it and set about making not coffee, but chocolate, which with a touch of brandy was the ultimate in comfort drinks. She took the mug, sipped it and smiled. 'Oh, that's good.'

'It's what my nanny made for me when I needed some serious comfort,' he said.

'She gave you brandy?'

'Just enough to scent the steam. Come on, snuggle

up,' he said, lifting his arm. 'You might as well have the whole comfort experience.'

She looked at him. 'You know, when I first saw you I thought you were the big bad giant straight out of my childhood nightmares.'

'Yes, I caught your description of me when you were talking to Vickie Campbell. I should have run then.'

'Run?'

'For my life. Everyone knows what Jack did to the giant.' He gestured with his head and, grinning, she snuggled against him. They sat in silence for a while, drinking the chocolate, the house settling around them, and gradually he felt the tension leave her. He thought he could be happy just sitting there with her, his arm around her, for the rest of his life, but there were demons to face and the sooner the better, so he took her mug, set it on the floor and said, 'Tell me about Emma, Jacqui.'

And she must have been ready to talk, because she didn't hesitate. 'I always loved children. My sisters are older than me, were well into single-handedly raising the birth rate by the time I went to university. Vickie Campbell knew them, had seen me with the brood and offered me the chance to work for her as a temp, a flying nanny, during the holidays.'

'How does that work? The flying bit?'

'Oh, I ferried kids about, the way I was supposed to with Maisie. Took over in emergencies when a nanny walked out, or a mother had to go into hospital.' She looked down into her cup. 'Or died.'

'That's what happened with Emma? Her mother died?'

She nodded. 'A car accident: Absolutely tragic. Her husband couldn't cope. She was so young, so angry because her mother had left her and she just didn't understand why. I was with them the whole summer and she was just about accepting me, opening up, beginning to trust me when it was time for me to go back to uni. What was I going to do? If I'd left her, she'd be losing the one person she could rely on for the second time in her short life. She'd never have believed in anyone ever again.'

He thought about how she'd been with Maisie. Standing her corner. Refusing to budge. And he said, 'No. I can see that you'd never leave anyone who needed you.'

'I never let her forget her mother, or tried to take her place, but she was just a face in a photograph, as insubstantial as an angel. In every practical way I was her mother. Her father, too, because he wasn't a lot of use. I promised her I'd always be there, that I'd never leave her.'

'What happened?'

'David Gilchrist was an investment banker. A wealthy, personable man. I'd been Emma's nanny for nearly four years when he brought home a woman he'd met on his travels and calmly informed me that they were married. And equally calmly told Emma that she had a new mother. Emma, confronted with a total stranger, declared roundly that I was the only mummy she ever wanted, at which point my feet didn't touch the ground. I was out of there faster than you can say wicked stepmother and in weeks they'd moved lock, stock and barrel to Hong Kong.'

'And the bracelet?'

'It was returned with a brief note reminding me that I had only ever been an employee and asking me not to contact Emma ever again. No birthday or Christmas presents. No cards. Nothing. The new Mrs Gilchrist even sent it to the agency rather than directly to me, just to rub home the point.'

'That was harsh.'

'Yes, it was, but I suppose she thought that if she didn't erase Emma's memory of me she'd never have her love, and perhaps she was right. The truth is that I became so emotionally involved that I forgot the first principle of being a nanny. The child you care for is not yours. You have to be prepared to let go...'

She blinked and a tear escaped, trickled down her nose. He wiped it away with the edge of his thumb. 'There are no rules when it comes to children. You love them because you can't help it and when you lose them it hurts.'

'You've got another chance with Maisie. Don't throw it away.'

'Thanks to you.'

'I think it was something of a combined effort, Harry.'

'But you were at the sharp end, taking the flak. How many women would have stayed?'

'Maisie was the one who wanted to stay.'

Only Maisie?

'So,' he said, trying to keep his voice steady, 'are you planning to fly away now you've done your Mary Poppins bit?'

'How? You've had my car towed away.' Then, looking up at him with the sparkle back in her eyes, 'And Maisie did promise me that I'd have a good time if I spent my holiday here.'

'And what did you promise her?'

'Just that I'd stay while she needs me, Harry. I've

learned my lesson. No more open-ended, forever promises.'

'None?'

She was tucked up against him, soft and yielding against his body, and her face was lifted towards him. He lifted his hand, not sure, desperately afraid, but he'd been running for so long. Now was the time to stand, say what he wanted.

Maisie back in his life.

A new way of living.

Jacqui.

'What if I was to say that I need you?' he asked.

'You don't know me, Harry.'

He touched her cheek, pushed her hair back from her face, fumbling like a boy trying to work out how to go about his first kiss. She regarded him with the steady look of a woman prepared to wait until he got it right.

'Your character shines out in everything you do. I'm the risk here, but I'm asking you to take a chance. Will you stay?'

'What are you asking?'

He answered her with the gentlest brush of his lips over hers. 'You know what I'm asking.'

There was the longest pause, a silence that seemed endless. It was shattered by the kitchen door being flung open. 'I've been shouting and shouting for a drink of water…' Then, seeing them wrapped in each other's arms, Maisie skidded to a halt and said, 'Oops.'

And that was it, the moment was over and Jacqui was already halfway across the kitchen, taking a glass from the cupboard, half filling it with water and handing it to Maisie.

'Come on, sweetpea, back to bed with you,' she said. 'We've got an early start in the morning.'

But Maisie refused to be hurried. She drank slowly, and then, when she'd finished, she looked directly at him, a tiny frown creasing her forehead, something clearly on her mind.

'Is there a problem?' he asked. He hoped she wasn't about to tell him she'd changed her mind about going to the village school. He'd begun to have this picture in his mind of them walking hand in hand through the school gates on her first day…

'You're my daddy, right?' she asked.

'Right,' he said, fighting the catch in his throat. How could he ever have doubted it? 'Right.'

'So, if you're kissing Jacqui, does that mean she's going to be my mummy?'

'You already have a mummy,' Jacqui said quickly, clearly intent on saving him from the embarrassment of answering that one.

'No.' Maisie wasn't so easily diverted. 'I have a *mother*,' she said. 'It's not the same.'

# CHAPTER ELEVEN

'WHAT'S the difference, Maisie?'

Harry leapt in before she could whisk Maisie upstairs and Jacqui felt as if she was walking on the edge of a precipice. One wrong step would mean disaster.

She'd be lying to herself if she pretended that she hadn't wanted Harry to kiss her, really kiss her. She'd wanted it since that instant of connection outside the stables when he'd been looking at her car. In that moment when all either of them could do was look...

There had been a kind of recognition, a primeval tug of whatever it was that made men and women fall into bed without a thought for the future. Honesty compelled her to admit she'd wanted a lot more than a kiss even then, but she knew how easy it was to get carried away by her emotions.

It would be so easy for her to imagine that what she felt, what Harry felt, was something more than a fleeting moment of attraction, desire. So easy to muddle her responsibility towards Maisie with what she felt for Harry.

As for Harry...he had to be in turmoil right now. The child he loved, the child he'd lost, pitched back into his lap without warning.

It would be so easy if a child's well-being wasn't involved, but she wouldn't allow herself to confuse her roles again. Hurt another little girl with promises that neither of them were sure they could keep.

Maisie, of course, had no such problem. She just

lifted her shoulders in a shrug that reached her ears and said, 'Mummies do stuff. Like finding the chicks, and cooking and having time to play. My mother is always busy. Always going away. Jacqui's like a mummy in a story book.'

Jacqui saw Harry's jaw tighten ominously and leapt in with, 'Well, right now Jacqui thinks you should be in bed.' She looked up. 'Right, Daddy?'

'Right.' And he was beside them in a heartbeat, sweeping Maisie up in his arms. 'Early to bed, early to rise… So that we can go shopping. School kit, yes? Still sure you want to go?'

Maisie giggled and Jacqui, whose first instinct was to follow them upstairs, paused at the kitchen door and, when her absence wasn't noticed, collected the tray from the library, washed the mugs.

Then she tidied the mud room, putting the boots in size order.

When, after that, Harry still hadn't reappeared, she went upstairs, glancing in at Maisie as she passed.

She'd fallen asleep while Harry read to her, but he hadn't moved, clearly unable to take his eyes off her. He'd said he was a risk, but there was nothing wrong with a man who could look at a child with such tenderness, such love and she apologised to her hormones for ever doubting their good taste. They clearly recognised a good man when they saw him.

After a moment, feeling like an intruder, she turned away. She'd done the job she been asked to do. Seen Maisie to a safe haven. It was time to leave.

'Don't go, Jacqui…'

She paused, glanced back. 'I didn't think you'd seen me.'

'I didn't need to see you. I felt your presence.' He

stood up, looked at Maisie for one long moment then joined her at the door. 'Don't go, Jacqui.'

About to ask how he knew what she was thinking, she decided against it. He'd been reading her thoughts since the moment she arrived; her only defence was not to think them.

'Maisie doesn't need me now,' she said. She was free of her promise. 'She has you.'

'And if I tell you again that I need you?'

She reminded herself that she'd made him no promises. That despite the unexpected appeal of a misty hilltop she was supposed to be in Spain. That all he needed, all he was asking for, was her help with Maisie.

'You're like all men,' she said, making light of it. 'You just can't handle shopping.'

His gaze didn't waver. 'Is that a yes?'

'I'll stay for a little while,' she conceded, knowing that she was a fool. Then, more to convince herself than because she believed it, 'Maisie's never been to school before. She might find it…challenging.'

'Is that a promise?'

He was standing close enough to touch, close enough to kiss. Just one would have been enough for her to swear her life away and, mind-reader that he was, she suspected that he knew it.

He did neither and she did it anyway.

'It's a promise.'

How long was a little while? When each moment was precious it seemed unbearably brief. She'd spent the day with Harry and Maisie shopping for 'ordinary' clothes. School kit first, then they'd got a bit carried away and bought a pile of the ordinary stuff that little girls needed. The kind of shoes that a child could play in. A pair of her own wellington boots in the right size to live in the mud room. Warm jackets, mini cargo trousers, T-shirts, socks...

'You know Maisie must have all this stuff at home,' she finally objected when yet another 'essential' was added to the shopping basket.

'Really?' Harry shook his head. 'I didn't notice anything like this at Hill Tops, did you?'

'No, I meant...' Then she caught on and very nearly hugged him. She restrained herself—she'd been doing rather too much of that in the last few days, which had to be bad, because she'd never felt the least desire to hug Emma's father—and instead put another pair of socks in the basket and contented herself with a smile.

He did not smile back. She swallowed and, unable to quite handle the directness of his gaze, turned to Maisie.

'Are you hungry?'

She did her best to steer everyone in the direction of proper food, but Maisie wanted a burger and Harry said, 'Just this once.' And that was that.

Just as it was 'that' when he overrode her insistence that he should be the one to take her to school the next day.

'We'll both go; that way the head teacher will know you.' Which was such a reasonable point that she couldn't possibly object.

But as Maisie, looking so small in her little grey skirt and red sweatshirt, walked away from them and was swallowed up in a throng of children eager to find out who she was, somehow their hands were interlinked in the tightest clasp.

'She'll be all right, won't she?' Harry asked, not looking at her.

'It's the other kids you should be worrying about,' she said, not looking at him as she blinked back a tear.

And OK, maybe she should have left after that first day, when Maisie hurtled out of school saying that it was, 'Brilliant!' And, 'Your name is on the mummys' reading rota and I'm going to be a fairy in the end-of-term play and you've both got to sit in the front row so that you can see me.'

But then Jacqui's sister called to see how she was enjoying her holiday and, when she explained what had happened, gave her a lecture about allowing herself to get sucked into caring for another child when she was supposed to be on holiday—all heavily laden with un-spoken but unmistakable never-learning-her-lesson overtones—and she was more than a little ticked off.

She wasn't staying forever.

Only until the end of school term.

No way would she swap the joy of seeing Maisie in her first school play for all the sangria in Spain.

And then Vickie phoned and said that Selina Talbot had faxed through a desperate apology, along with per-mission for her to leave Maisie with Harry.

'No need to stay a day longer, darling. I've been on to the travel agents and they're getting back to me with flight times this afternoon. Selina's paying for up-grades, too.'

'That's kind of her, but actually, Vickie,' she said, 'I think I'll give Spain a miss this year. I like it here.'

'But you can't stay!'

'I *can't*?'

'Selina is very unhappy that you stayed. She won't pay you for another day.'

'Vickie—darling—I can do what I like. I don't work for you or Selina Talbot.' And she hung up.

She looked up, knowing that Harry would be there. He was leaning against the door, something close to a smile lighting his eyes. Almost laughing, but not quite.

'It's just until the end of term,' she said primly. 'I can't miss the school play.'

'Maisie will be pleased.'

And what about you, Harry Talbot? she asked herself.

But he wasn't saying anything. Wasn't flinging himself at her. No more reaching out for her. No more 'comfort' in a mug of hot chocolate.

He was just there.

Driving them both to school every morning, although the potholes had been filled in and her car was back in the coach house so she could easily have done it herself.

A fixture at mealtimes. Breakfast with Maisie, then, after the school run, appearing at lunchtime from the yard, or the fields, or the library, ready to share a sandwich if she'd made one. Ready to make one and share it with her if she'd been busy helping Susan.

Pushing the cart around the supermarket when she wanted to go shopping and quite happy to demonstrate that he could cook as well as she could when the fancy took him.

He didn't disappear the minute supper was done, either, but stayed to help with the clearing up, chatting to Maisie about her day. Making coffee. Joining in the ritual of bath times and taking turns with her reading bedtime stories.

She'd hung back, sure that he would want this special time all to himself, but he'd insisted.

And once Maisie was in bed they spent the evenings in the library in front of the fire, reading, music playing softly in the background.

Maisie was right. Hill Tops was a wonderful place to stay now that the mist had evaporated and the sky was a clear eggshell-blue against the beauty of the valley.

There were daffodils and lambs everywhere and, besides, someone had to keep an eye on those stupid chickens who would keep going broody and laying their eggs in secret, oblivious to the dangers in their desperation to hatch their chicks.

But it was Harry, looking up and meeting her eyes, as he turned the page of a book; Harry, helping Maisie with her spellings; Harry, matching his long stride to Maisie's little legs as they walked the hills so that he could teach her the names of wild flowers who made it the place she never wanted to leave.

'I had an email from Aunt Kate this morning,' he said. It was the last day of term and they were driving down to the school to watch the school play. Neither of them had said anything about her leaving in the morning, but she'd packed her bag so that she had no excuse to delay.

She was glad she had. It was going to be hard enough without dragging it out and this sounded very much like a hint that her 'little while' was up.

'Did she say when she's coming home?'

'No. She likes New Zealand and she doesn't want to leave her sister. She's staying on indefinitely.'

'Oh.' Then, forgetting her own feelings as she realised what this must mean, 'Oh! Will she sell the house? Will you have to find somewhere else to live?'

'Would that worry you?'

'Me? Why are you asking me?'

'Because it's important to me. I want to know how you feel.'

'Maisie loves it.'

'That's a major consideration,' he agreed. 'What about you? Do you love it here, too? Despite the chickens.'

'I'm getting used to the chickens,' she said, carefully. 'But that's a consideration, too, isn't it? What will happen to the animals if you leave?'

'The pleasure of telling Sally that she'll have to find new homes for those wretched donkeys might be worth it.'

'Sure,' she said, going for a matching grin and falling way short. If the feeling didn't come from inside, nothing could make a smile look right. 'You're so hard.' Then, 'It's a wonderful place to live, Harry, but it's the people that make a place special.'

'I think so,' he agreed.

'What will you do if you go?'

'The right question, Jacqui, is what will I do if I stay?'

'OK, that, too.'

'I was thinking about reopening the medical practice in the village. With new houses, more people, there's a need.'

'Then you've answered your own question. It's your family home. Maisie's your family. And there's plenty of room for her mother to visit when she…'

'When she needs some new photographs for some celebrity magazine?'

'I was going to say when she's feeling maternal. I'm sure she loves Maisie in her own way.'

'Yes, of course she does.' Then, 'Oh, good grief, we should have set off earlier.'

The village was packed with cars, four-wheel drives and trucks parked nose to tail. Even the pub car park was overflowing and Harry took the last place as he squeezed the Land Rover into a space opposite the church.

Only then did he turn to her and say, 'I have one more.'

'What?'

'Question.'

'Harry—'

'In the light of your assertion that people are more important than places, will you stay?'

She was prevented—saved—from having to answer him by her mobile phone. 'It'll be the t-temp agency,' she stuttered, fumbling for it in her bag. 'I called them and asked them to find me something for next week.'

'Unpack your bag, Jacqui,' he said, taking the phone from her before she could even see the caller ID. He turned it off, put it in his jacket pocket. 'You don't need a temporary job. I'm offering you one for the rest of your life. All you have to do is say yes. But not now.' He climbed out, opened the passenger door. 'Come on,' he said, lifting her down as if she were a feather. 'Maisie will never forgive us if we're late.'

It was as well that he was there to help her down. Her legs were so shaky that she'd never have made it on her own.

Stay? For the rest of her life?


The afternoon was a joy. The little ones portrayed nursery rhymes—Bo Peep's lamb was the genuine article, which was, Jacqui thought, courageous. It was perhaps

just as well that the teacher stopped there and that the
cow jumping over the moon was made of cardboard.
Someone stood on Wee Willie Winkie's nightgown
and the seam gave way, leaving him standing in his
tiny Y-fronts. And the house that Jack built fell down.
Maisie, in full fairy fig, complete with wings and wand
as the fairy who brought them all to life, was a star.

It was an age before they could finally get away.
Everyone wanted to say hello, invite Maisie to play.
Harry in turn announced an Easter-egg hunt at Hill
Tops, which had Maisie whooping with excitement and
demanding every detail on the way home. Was it like
a party? Would Jacqui make a cake? Could *everyone*
come?

By the time they reached the top of the lane she was
wrung out. This was so unfair. She was being manip-
ulated, backed into a corner by Harry. If he needed her
to stay and look after Maisie he should just come out
and say so. And she could say no.

'We seem to have visitors,' Harry said as he slowed.
'The gate's open.'

'Who...?' And then she saw 'who' and she was
flinging herself from the Land Rover before he brought
it to a stop. Scooping up the small girl who, fair hair
flying behind her, hurtled into her arms.

'Emmy! My darling! What are you doing here?'
Then she looked at the Gilchrists, standing beside their
car, looking desperate, and knew why they were there.
At which point, heart sinking, she knew there was only
one answer to Harry's question. She wanted to stay but
she was about to be called on a promise.

She put Emma down, although the child continued
to cling to her hand, and encouraged Maisie—who had
instantly claimed the other—to take Emma to see her

pony. Emma was sufficiently impressed by the fact that Maisie had a pony to allow herself to be persuaded to let go.

Then she introduced the Gilchrists to Harry.

'Harry, this is Jessica and David Gilchrist. I used to work for David as Emma's nanny.'

'Jacqui told me all about you,' he said. His smile wouldn't have fooled anyone who knew him. And, producing a key for the front door—which, although they didn't know it, put them firmly in their place; friends never used the front door in the country—he invited them in. 'There's a fire in the library; why don't you make yourselves comfortable while I make some tea?'

David Gilchrist lifted his eyebrows, clearly unimpressed by a man who made tea for visitors when he had an employee at hand to do it for him.

The new Mrs Gilchrist just looked desperate.

'Jacqui,' she said, as soon as Harry had gone, 'I've made a terrible mistake. Can you ever forgive me?'

'Of course. You didn't need to come all this way to tell me that.' She anticipated denials that they'd flown from Hong Kong specifically for the purpose. When she didn't get them, her heart sank even further. 'How did you know where I was?'

'Mrs Campbell told us. She said she was going to phone and let you know we were on our way.'

'My cellphone was switched off. We've been at Maisie's school play. I hope you didn't have to wait too long.'

She shook her head as if it didn't matter. 'You are so good with children.'

'There's no magic to it, Jessica. They're people, just like the rest of us.'

'You make it sound so easy. Emma...' She shook

her head, staring at her hands as they twisted her scarf into a knot. 'I can't cope with her. She hates me. I'm asking you, begging you to come back. She told me that you promised her you'd always be there if she needed you.' Then, as if aware that she'd stepped over some invisible line, 'You'll have your own flat, your own car, we'll pay whatever you ask. Hong Kong is a wonderful place—'

Jacqui covered her hand, stopping her. 'Do you think that after what happened I could, would, ever do this for money again?'

Jessica looked up then, confused. 'But you're here. Mrs Campbell said that it was just temporary. We're offering you a good, permanent job—'

'You heard her, Mrs Gilchrist. Jacqui is not for hire. And, despite anything Mrs Campbell might have told you, she's not Maisie's nanny.'

All three of them turned to look at Harry standing in the doorway, a tray in his hands.

'Then what is she?' David Gilchrist demanded.

'To Maisie she's her proper mummy. To me—' he paused, looked straight at her, spoke straight to her '—she's the light at the end of a long, dark tunnel. Warmth on a cold winter's night. Comfort. Joy. Quite simply she makes my world complete.'

Jacqui was barely conscious of David Gilchrist's knowing, 'I see.'

Harry's soft, 'No, Gilchrist, you haven't the slightest idea.'

'We're wasting our time here, Jessica. There are hundreds of nannies looking for the kind of job we're offering.'

'Haven't you learned anything?' Harry, asked, dangerously quiet. 'Caring for a child isn't just a job—'

David Gilchrist got to his feet and, taking his wife's arm, said, 'Let's go.'

Jacqui leapt to her feet. 'No! Wait…' She turned to Harry, silently pleading for him to understand.

And Harry Talbot, who had laid his raw, unprotected heart on the line to keep her at his side, knew it was going to be broken all over again.

Then she said, 'Harry, will you take David and check on the children? Make sure they're not getting into any trouble? I need to talk to Jessica.'

'I thought you were going with them.'

'Because I promised?' Jacqui, leaning on the gate to watch the Gilchrists' car out of sight, waving one last time to Emma, reached back for his hand.

He took it gladly. Held it as if he would never let it go.

'Because you promised,' he said.

'Emma doesn't need me. She has a mummy. Someone who'll care for her because she loves her, not because there's a cheque in the bank every month.'

'Oh, right, the way you did.'

'David Gilchrist is wealthy, good-looking in a stuffed-shirt sort of way, still young. It's inevitable that he would remarry.'

'With you in the house I can't imagine why he ever looked further.'

She laughed. 'Oh, please. I was the hired help. He probably thinks I've found my level with a…what did he call you?'

'A gentleman farmer.'

'You didn't correct him.'

'I didn't think he was worth the breath.' Then, 'So

is Emma content? Did the bracelet compensate her for losing you?'

'She hasn't lost me. She understands that now. She just needed to know that I hadn't deserted her, Harry. Poor Jessica Gilchrist panicked, thought she had to eradicate me totally from their lives before Emma would love her. She didn't understand that a child's love is boundless.'

'It's that simple?'

'No. It'll take time, but I said she could call for a chat any time.'

'From Hong Kong?'

'They can afford it.'

'And what did you tell Emma?'

'That I'd always love her. That I'll always be there when she needs me. I don't have to live in the same house, or even the same country, for that to be true. All she has to do is pick up a phone.'

'You said she can call any time, too?'

'Actually, Harry, I did rather more than that. I said she could come and stay in the summer. Do you mind?'

Mind? If Emma was coming it meant that Jacqui would be there.

'The only thing I care about is whether you're staying. I thought for a moment back there that I'd lost you.'

'Did you?' She looked up at him, eyes steady as a rock. 'And would you have let me go as easily as Maisie?'

'No, my love. The Gilchrists were offering you a job. I'm offering you my life. All that I have.'

'Tell me about the future, Harry,' she asked, her voice catching like cobwebs in her throat. 'About the rest of our lives.'

'Being the wife of a country doctor is not the softest option,' he said. 'Nothing like the luxurious lifestyle you'd get in Hong Kong.' She gave his arm a playful punch. 'And I know how you dislike chickens…'

'I'm getting used to the chickens and, excuse me, but was that a proposal?'

'You want me on my knees?'

She looked down. There was still a muddy patch in the dip at the centre of the drive, but she took pity on him and said, 'Why don't we save that for later? When you're showing me exactly what you meant by that "warmth on a winter night", thing.'

'It's not winter, my love. The sun is shining. Next Sunday is Easter.'

She gave a little shiver. 'I've seen snow at Easter.'

'Well, now you come to mention it, you could be right. We'll probably get a frost tonight.' He put his arm around her as they walked back to the house. 'Anything else I can do for you?'

'Well, I really hate that "keep out" sign on the gate.'

'I'll get a screwdriver right now.'

'And we should have a goat, don't you think?'

'A goat?' He laughed. 'Have you ever tried to milk a goat?'

'No, but surely it's mandatory?' He must have looked puzzled. 'Every smallholding has to have one.'

'What makes you think this is a smallholding?'

'Two fields, five donkeys, one pony and I've lost count of the chickens and rabbits.'

He stopped. 'Look around you.' She glanced around. 'No, right around. To the summit of the hill, as far as you can see to left and right. Down as far as the main road.'

He saw light dawning in her eyes. 'All that? But that includes the village.'

'It was part of the original estate, but my grandfather gave the villagers their freeholds about fifty years ago. Most of the land is leased to local farmers.'

'But it's huge! Can you afford to buy it from your aunt?'

'At today's prices I might be struggling, but I bought it from Aunt Kate ten years ago when she wanted to finance Sally's career.'

'But she stayed on?'

'Nothing changed but the ownership. I gave her the legal authority to manage everything as she'd always done and I have to say that she did a good job. I've only just discovered that she made me a small fortune by selling off a field close to the village for building land. With the village expanding, there'll be more. I'll have to renegotiate the price I paid her to reflect that.' He smiled down at her. 'Still want a goat?'

'Can I upgrade that to a pony for Maisie? One that won't expire if she sits on it.'

'I thought we might get her one for her birthday.'

We.

Jacqui thought it was the most beautiful word she'd ever heard and, linking her arm through his, she said, 'Perfect.'

'She could probably do with some brothers and sisters, too.'

She glanced up at him. 'That's long-term planning.'

'Since it's going to be a cold night, we could make a start right away if you like.' He stopped, took her in his arms. 'On the planning. Starting with a date for the wedding.' Then, after a long, lingering kiss that left her in no doubt of his feelings, left her in no doubt of hers, he said, 'Don't let's wait too long.'

June, everyone agreed, was the perfect month for a country wedding. The church had been decorated with flowers courtesy of Selina Talbot in lieu of her presence. She'd married her billionaire and wasn't interrupting her honeymoon for anyone, not even for Maisie, who had a lead role as bridesmaid.

The lane needed no help. Nature herself had decorated for their special day with white frilly billows of cow parsley, foxgloves, the glowing yellow of tall buttercups.

The posse of small bridesmaids—Maisie and Emma and Jacqui's nieces, circlets of flowers woven into their hair—was driven down to the church in a trap pulled by a smart little pony.

Jacqui followed a couple of minutes later with her father in another, the harness bedecked with hedgerow flowers.

'You really didn't mind me not getting married from home?' she asked.

Her father squeezed her hand. 'This is your home, Jacqui. I've never seen you happier.'

'I'm so grateful to you and Mum for staying to take care of Maisie while we're away.'

'This is a magical place, sweetheart. We'll have the time of our lives.'

If the promises were solemn, till-death-us-do-part vows that were pledged not just with the ancient words, but with their eyes, hearts, souls, the revelries that followed were not.

There was no ceremony about the wedding breakfast. The food was laid out in a huge marquee in the flattest field on the estate and everyone just helped themselves. The dancing owed nothing to loud disco music, everything to a group of fiddlers who played reels and jigs that not even the most laid-back teenager could resist.

It went on long after the principle characters had slipped away to begin their honeymoon, a celebration of life, love, all the simple pleasures.

As the lady who ran the village shop said to the vicar's wife—after several glasses of champagne—it was as if the village had come back to life after a very long winter.

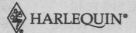

# HARLEQUIN ROMANCE®

## Coming Next Month

### #3875 HER SPANISH BOSS Barbara McMahon
*9 to 5*

When Rachel Goodson starts working for Luis Alvares, he's prickly and suspicious. But soon they draw closer and secrets spill out. Luis's heart is still with his late wife, so Rachel is stunned when he wants her to pose as his girlfriend. Then Luis makes it clear he wants more than just a pretend relationship....

### #3876 IN THE ARMS OF THE SHEIKH Sophie Weston

Natasha Lambert is horrified by what she must wear as her best friend's bridesmaid! Worse, the best man is Kazim al Saraq—an infuriatingly charming sheikh with a dazzling wit and an old-fashioned take on romance. He's determined to win Natasha's heart—and Natasha is terrified he might succeed...!

### #3877 A BRIDE WORTH WAITING FOR Caroline Anderson
*Heart to Heart*

Annie Shaw believes her boyfriend, Michael Harding, died in a brutal attack nine years ago. Little does she know that he has been forced to live undercover. Now Michael is free to pick up his life and reveal himself to the woman he loves. Can Annie fall in love with the man he has become?

### #3878 A FAMILY TO BELONG TO Natasha Oakley

Once, Kate loved Gideon from afar—but he was married and had the kind of family life Kate knew she could never have. Now, years later, Kate meets Gideon again—bringing up his children alone. They long to get close—but that will mean finding the courage to confront the past...and find a future.